DETERRENT

Deborah Greenspan

From a story
by Scott Van Gundy

Llumina Press

Requests for permission to make copies of any part of this work should be mailed to Permissions Department, Llumina Press, PO Box 772246, Coral Springs, FL 33077-2246

ISBN: 1-59526-491-4

Printed in the United States of America by Llumina Press

Library of Congress Control Number: 2005907552

DETERRENT

NEXT YEAR

Chapter One

Just a little closer . . . come on come on . . . just a little closer . . . " For a moment, the man who spoke could see himself hiding in the woods as if he were outside himself, as if he were Father. There was the little wooded area lining the main road, and there *he* was—a mysterious figure shrouded in leafy shadows, waiting. He adjusted his position behind the tree, and kept his mouth closed so the words would stay inside. The boy was almost upon him. He didn't want to lose him now.

Every day, he watched the boy take this same shortcut through the woods to the residential street on the other side. Every day, he followed the child from the moment he entered the woods until he exited five minutes later. Few boys braved the mysteries of the woods, preferring to go around, but his chosen was as reliable as clockwork.

He had been watching the boy for a long time. "Bye Ricky," another boy called, turning to cross the street.

"Hello Ricky," the man whispered. Ricky? What kind of name was that? The boy's name wasn't Ricky; it was Jeffy. He was sure it was Jeffy. The leaves rustled. He stepped out into the path.

"'Scuse me," the kid said and tried to go around him.

The man smiled and moved to block him again. This was a fun game. Every time the boy tried to go past, he moved to stop him.

"Hey! Get outta my way!" The kid was getting panicky.

He knew how that felt, and he laughed because he wasn't scared; it was Jeffy who was scared this time. Jeffy tried to push him out of the way, but he was bigger. He moved back into the cover of the trees and pulled Jeffy with him. Green leaves edged with yellow closed them in.

The boy sure could struggle! He was kicking, scratching, and hitting. Whoa! Look out there! This was fun! He wanted to make it last. Holding the boy at arm's length, he giggled at the wild swings that failed to connect. Then he let go. Suddenly, Jeffy realized he was free. He pulled away, and turned to run.

Father watched it as if it were happening in slow motion. The boy raced through the trees, and he followed, branches slapping at his face and catching on his clothes. Then he took a few of those big strides of his, closing the distance and trapping the kid against a thicket. Jeffy scuttled into the brambles, but the man hauled him out. His eyes followed the red line trickling like a tear down the boy's face.

"Lemme go! Please! Please lemme go!" The boy's face was all wet and slimy. His nose was dripping. Yuck. He hated that. Angry now, he shoved the kid away from him, watching coldly as he landed on his ass. Still sniveling, he scrambled backwards.

"Come on," the man suggested, "try to run away."

Jeffy didn't wait for a second challenge. He leapt to his feet and sprinted toward safety. But the man knew there was nowhere he could hide. He chased the boy through the trees and pinned him against an oak. Jeffy struggled, even trying to kick him in the vitals, but he was too small. "I'm bigger than you now, see?"

The knife came out of his pocket and the boy's eyes grew wide. Was he afraid? Didn't he know it was just a game?

◆ ◆ ◆

John Wallace looked around the empty room, the scuffed and dirty linoleum making a fitting support for bare tables, fallen placards, and ragged bunting. They had tried. He had tried. He sat with his head in his hands feeling the entire weight of his sixty years. The last stragglers picked up their belongings, whispered their goodbyes into the funereal air, and exited the scene. Wallace sighed.

Their setback was real, and it was hard to generate excitement under such a crushing defeat. Tomorrow, they'd rally perhaps, but tonight there was nothing to do but go home, have a drink, and go to bed. Some of his volunteers might have a good cry first. Hell, he might have a good cry.

Jack Decker came up to the table and offered his hand. "Hey Doc, don't let it get you down." Decker had that strong, determined look that made you want to trust him, and he hadn't changed at all since college, Wallace noted. He reached for his former student's hand—a lifeline—and shook it gratefully. "Are you coming to the rally?"

"Bet your ass!" Jack saluted and headed for the door, stepping aside as it opened and let James Farrell into the room.

Wallace watched the District Attorney approach, waiting as he pulled up a folding chair and sat down opposite.

Farrell looked around at the evidence of defeat, and sighed. "Maybe it's time to quit."

Wallace made an attempt at laughter. "James, have you ever seen me give up? Throw in the towel on the court? Back down from any man? . . . Why do you think I would walk away from the biggest fight of my life?"

Farrell shook his head. "I never thought that law would pass. I swear. I thought the Senate would throw it out. Now I wish I'd been more help."

Wallace got up and started to pace. "It's not too late. You can still make a difference. I know you're supposed to be tough on crime and all that politically correct crap, but this goes beyond politics. This is about good and . . . "

Farrell tipped the chair back, looked at the ceiling and painfully expelled the words. "Nothing goes beyond politics, Doc. Not in this world."

Wallace had known James Farrell for years, ever since he'd testified as an expert witness for the prosecution when Farrell was just coming up the ranks. They'd hit it off from the start, and their mutual love of tennis had cemented their relationship. In some ways, Wallace knew he was a father figure, Farrell's own having disappeared when he was just a kid, but that only added to their relationship. He'd been trying to recruit the D.A. to the S.E.E. movement for months. The younger man was on their side ideologically, but Farrell would have to risk his career to take the position Wallace was asking him to take. And now time had run out. With the signing of the proposal into law, every closet supporter had to become an active participant. "Are you going to help?"

"I don't know. I want to . . . but everyone is pressuring me to call for the Eye-for-an-Eye, and to tell you the truth, I can't see a way out."

Wallace watched Farrell's eyes. They slid off his own and lit on the torn bunting. Farrell was like that cloth—trying to go in two directions at once. If Wallace could only figure out a way to get him to choose, he'd be a powerful ally. The D.A., after all, though strong on crime prevention, could see that murdering murderers was just another step on the road to total chaos.

◆ ◆ ◆

James Farrell didn't look up when Paul Trevino entered his office; his eyes were fixed on the scene unfolding on the six o'clock news. He raised the remote to make it louder. It was difficult to believe what he was seeing. Right there, in living color, civilization was crumbling.

"Hey! James!" Trevino slapped his hand on the desk and slumped into a seat. Farrell glanced at him. He'd probably like a bag of popcorn to go with the spectacle, he thought. Then he turned back to the TV and the governor's speech.

"Today, I believe we've made real strides in our battle against violent crime in this state. We've tried other measures, safer measures, less drastic measures, and they've had little effect. Today, we're making changes. Let every criminal be warned: The State of Texas will no longer execute you if you commit murder. That privilege will go to the relatives of the victims, and you can be sure that people so deeply wronged will not let any murderer go "gently into the night . . . "

The reporters on the screen went wild. Questions were hurled from every direction.

"Governor, is it true that the new law makes it impossible for a murderer to appeal?"

The governor smiled grimly. "Not at all, son. The Eye-for-an-Eye law limits appeals to 30 days. If a convicted murderer does not file an appeal in time, he forfeits his right to do so at a later date."

"But, governor," another reporter called out, "aren't you afraid some people will be unjustly punished?"

The governor looked thoughtful. At another time, Farrell might have cynically noted the politician's repertoire of carefully thought out "looks." But not now. "Safeguards are built into the law—DNA testing for example—so no, I'm not worried about that. And I've never heard it said," the leader continued, "nor have I ever read, that justice cannot be done swiftly. In Texas, we will no longer allow murderers years in which to appeal."

"What about the 8th amendment? Doesn't the law violate the 8th amendment?"

The governor sat up straighter and looked dead serious. "In this great country, our system of justice is carefully protected by a series of checks and balances. If a bill is passed by the Texas Congress and signed into law by the executive—that's me," he smiled, "it's then up to the courts to decide on the constitutionality of that law, and to repeal it if necessary."

The governor was sharp. Farrell had to give him that. He handled the reporters like pets, rewarding them with approving smiles whenever they asked the questions he wanted to answer. Farrell couldn't stand it; he grabbed the nearest thing at hand—a sheaf of papers—and threw it at the television set. Then he got up and switched it off.

"Unbelievable," he muttered. "What the hell are you grinning at, Trevino?"

Captain Trevino, looking every bit of his fifty-nine years, was smiling like the Cheshire Cat. "Come off it, Farrell. This is great. Now these scum'll get what they deserve."

Farrell wished he had a dime for every time Trevino equated justice with revenge. He just didn't seem to understand that they were different concepts. And now, it appeared that the world, or at least the State of Texas, had vindicated the sloppiness of his thinking. "Are you crazy? What about due process? What about the 8th amendment? The fucking law is unconstitutional, and you know it!"

Trevino shrugged, one of his trademark red suspenders slipping off a massive shoulder. The one with the badge pinned on it, Farrell noted. The captain grinned. "But they passed it."

"Sure they passed it, and it will be overturned by the Supreme Court. But that could take years."

"So? In the meantime, we get to see justice done, don't we? Aren't you sick of seeing murderers walk? Come on! This is politics. The people who elected you want this law."

Farrell sagged into his seat. That was the crux of the whole issue really. He was the prosecutor. He picked up a small statue of blindfolded Justice and set her in front of him on the desk. "Oh, so you're saying the voters lobbied that travesty of a law into existence?" Glancing up, he saw Trevino shrug again.

"And did the voters also suspend their right to privacy and put up surveillance cameras everywhere? Did the voters decide to suspend the 4th amendment and allow illegal search and seizure? What do the voters have to do with this?" With each point, he'd placed something on the scale, and now, overbalanced, the figure toppled over.

Farrell met Trevino's eyes, knowing it was useless. Trying to get the captain to see past the brutality of the streets to the brutality that could be the law was like trying to get a vampire to drink milk. "Everywhere we turn we're losing our constitutional rights, and it's not the voters who are calling the shots."

"With all the violent crime we live with? Who else?"

"Someone will profit from the passage of this law," Farrell growled.

"Maybe so, but the voters are easily led. They believe it's their decision, and if you like your job, you'd better be prepared to give those voters what they think they want. It's simple arithmetic."

"I love my job. And I hate crime as much as you do. This law turns us all into criminals." Farrell hated this argument. They'd been having some version of it ever since Eye-for-an-Eye had been proposed. He was about to make another point when the door opened and Ginny Ormond walked in. Trevino looked like he was having a small heart attack. But he always looked like that when Ginny was around. Well, who could blame him?"

"Excuse me, Mr. Farrell, Captain Trevino, but it's after six, and I am required by my boss to remind him that he has to be in court in the morning."

Farrell laughed, and so did Ginny and the captain. She has a gift for doing that, thought Farrell, for releasing the tension in a room.

The captain sighed and got to his feet. "Well, I gotta push off myself. And you better get some rest, son. I hope you're not gonna go soft on old Sam-the-Slasher tomorrow."

"We've lined up a great jury," Ginny contributed. "Sam doesn't stand a chance."

"Oh yeah, prosecute him, Farrell. And make sure you call for an Eye-for-an-Eye. You hear?"

Farrell was well aware that Trevino wasn't going to leave without getting the last word, so he prudently kept his mouth shut and watched as the police captain exited his office, sparing one last fervent glance at Ginny before the door closed behind him.

Ginny's bright black eyes watched the door slip into the frame then turned to meet his. Holding his gaze, she slid around the desk and into his lap. Her arms went around his neck and her lips sought his.

"Now, Mr. District Attorney, didn't we have plans for tonight?" she whispered against his throat.

Farrell sank into her inviting embrace. "Hmm. I think we did . . . "

◆ ◆ ◆

Farrell's apartment, in contrast to his office, was filled with playthings: bikes, skates, weights, catcher's mitt, games, tennis racquet, racquetball racquet, tennis balls, racquet balls, baseball, basketball, soccer ball, volleyball, and every other type of ball known to man. If it was a game, and it was played on the ground, Farrell was in.

The contemporary black leather sofa, glass tables, and cherrywood furniture created a manly backdrop to Farrell's personal playground that didn't fool Ginny Ormond one bit. She knew she was dealing in some ways with a large boy, but that was what she liked about Farrell. He was spontaneous. He knew how to have a good time. And he was great in bed.

At least, he was usually great in bed: easily excited, eager to please, sensual, generous, and intelligent. Tonight, however, he seemed distracted. She sat up, the strap of her silken teddy slipping off her shoulder. "What's wrong?"

Farrell slipped a hand behind that shoulder and pulled her toward him. "Nothing," he said. "Come on. Nothing's wrong."

Ginny resisted. "You're not here, James."

Farrell's gaze turned inward momentarily, then he too sat up. Obviously, she'd struck a chord. "Sorry, Gin," he was saying, "I'm just not with it tonight."

Not much fun for her with him in this mood. She considered her options as she watched him lean over and pick up a baseball and mitt from the floor beside the bed. She liked watching him. He had a compact body with well-defined muscles moving under smooth skin—like a boxer. And she really dug the light brown hair and blue eyes. It was nice to be with someone so attractive. And it didn't hurt that he was the D.A.

James threw the ball into the air and caught it in the mitt, a routine she'd witnessed many times before. "It's just this Eye-for-an-Eye thing . . . . Doesn't it bother you?"

Ginny stretched like a cat, the red silk of her lingerie sliding sensuously across her skin. "No. Why? Should it?"

Farrell turned the full force of his eyes on her. "I've been against it from the beginning," he said. "I don't want to call for it; I don't want to ask the jury to use it."

Ginny couldn't believe what she was hearing. "What? Are you crazy? People want it. They want Sam-the-Slasher and others like him to get what they deserve."

The ball went up and came down, marking time, and Farrell's eyes followed the ellipse created by its motion. "I don't believe that."

Ginny's mouth dropped open, momentarily. Then she pulled herself together and stood up. When she was agitated it was impossible to stay still. "Why in hell not? You think the bill passed because people *didn't* want it?"

Farrell got up and followed her as she moved across the room. "Listen. Let's be real. Do people really have a lot to say about what laws are passed? I don't believe people want us to become as violent as the criminals we prosec . . . "

Rounding on him, Ginny's voice rose half an octave. "Come off it! People elected you to do a job. Now, do it."

She watched her words deflate him and took some satisfaction from her power as he slumped back onto the bed.

"Oh, I'll do it, but I won't like it," he muttered.

Sitting down next to him, she took his hand in hers and brought it to her lips. "Well, that's why they call it work, James. Until now it's all been gravy for you. I guess it's pay-back time."

She nuzzled his neck, breathing in the scent of masculinity overlaid with hints of her own perfume. Maybe now that he'd gotten it off his chest, he'd be more . . . interesting. She kissed him deeply, biting softly at his lower lip, but when she opened her eyes to look at him, she saw that he still wasn't paying attention.

"So work is doing what you hate and don't believe in, in order to keep doing the things you like?" he asked.

Ginny sighed. "Something like that." In another effort to get him out of his head and into his body, she released the strings holding up the wispy silk of her teddy so that it slid down the curves of her breasts.

His response was disappointing. "How can you like anything if most of the time you do what you hate?"

She snuggled closer, feeling the rounds of her bare flesh sliding against the skin of his chest and belly. Her voice was throaty as she whispered against his ear. "It has to do with being an adult. I mean, look at me. I don't want to spend the rest of my life in a district attorney's office, but I do it."

Farrell took her face in his hands and held her eyes with his. "Ginny, I know you had a tough childhood, but life isn't all that simple."

She shook him off and sat up.

"You don't like yourself much, do you?" he said.

"I like myself just fine! It's the rest of the human race . . . the greedy, bloodsucking, violent, selfish . . . "

Farrell was watching her, and she didn't like the look on his face. Carefully, she reined in her anger. "Well, I like people," he was saying, "I don't think we're as bad as you imagine."

Oh this was too much. "Are you saying you believe in . . . what? Goodness? That people are good?" His eyes said it all. "You do!"

"Okay, I do. What's wrong with that?"

Ginny was on her feet again, striding up and down the room. "It's a load of crap, that's what's wrong with it. You don't believe me? Ask my sister how it feels to be gang-raped at thirteen. No, Farrell, you're better off believing in numbers. As in votes . . . or money. If you don't call for an *Eye-for-an-Eye* for Sam-the-Slasher, you can bet your last dollar you won't be re-elected. It's political suicide!"

His face was unreadable, and she was sick of the whole conversation. Picking up her stockings, she sat on the bed as far from Farrell as she could get and drew them up her legs. The rest of her clothes were on the dresser, and she wasted no time retrieving them.

Farrell was still talking, but she was trying not to listen.

" . . . don't believe people want this law. More likely, someone's getting their pockets lined."

Oh, how could he be so dense? "Oh, I see," she said as she cinched the leather belt tight around her waist. "But didn't you just say that you believe people are good?"

"Come on. You know what I mean. We're not all bad."

"I'm going home, James. Call me when you grow up."

She didn't turn to see his face as she walked out. It was always better to leave men at a disadvantage, and she was good at that. Slamming the door behind her, she was sure that what followed was the satisfying thud of a baseball hitting the wood.

September 6ᵀᴴ - 8:43 PM

Billy (the Kid) Maxwell led his team of raiders into battle. "Aargh!" he screamed as his bike plunged into the brush. The others followed close behind. It was almost dark and Billy knew he wasn't supposed to enter the woods, but shit, he was the Captain now and his marauders would follow him anywhere!

"Come on!" he shouted, signaling with his arm for the men behind him to attack. The fallen leaves crackled beneath the wheels of their bikes as they moved off the trail and into the brush. Branches whipped across Billy's face. He could hardly see, but suddenly something was blocking his passage through the bushes. It had a menacing air that brought him to a standstill. The others piled into him.

"Shit!"

"What're ya doin?"

Billy held up a hand for silence. Getting off his bike, he moved slowly toward the bundle of rags lying on the ground. There was a rusty smell in the air.

"What is it, Billy?"

"Shut up, Parker," Derek ordered.

"Who's gonna make me?"

The boys followed Billy, bickering as they moved deeper into the shadows.

He didn't like the look of it. It looked like something bad in a movie. And what happened next was you turned it over and . . . "

"Ohmigod! Ohmigod!"

The boys ran screaming from the wood, from the bundle of rags that had turned out to be—just like in the movies—a bloody, glassy-eyed corpse.

Chapter Two

September 6th - 11:13 PM

P olice lights were flashing, spitting sparks of red, yellow, white, and blue into the surrounding dark. John Wallace pulled his car as close to the scene as he could get and sat for a moment, watching. There were half a dozen police cars parked every which way, an ambulance, people milling around craning their necks to get a look behind the yellow tape marking off the boundaries of the site, cops, rescue workers. It was organized bedlam.

In a moment, he'd get out of the car and his life would change completely in as yet undefined ways, but he wanted to hold that moment off for as long as he could. He took a deep breath and prayed briefly for it all to go away. Then he spotted Lindsey flanked by police, scrambling toward the ambulance. He got out and headed toward her.

She was crying, screaming with grief and pain.

"Lindsey," Wallace said.

She turned and he could see straight into her broken heart. "John! Oh John!" She threw her arms around him. He held her, felt her heart beating against his chest, her tears on his cheek.

He didn't want to know what had etched that pain into her soul. He tried not to know, but as he held her, the knowledge seeped into his heart.

"No!" he cried, his heart twisting with fear. "No. No."

Attendants wheeled the stretcher toward the ambulance. On it was a small body covered with a sheet. And under that sheet, Wallace knew, was his life. Lindsey grabbed the stretcher and reached for the body, but he took her hand and wouldn't let her pull down the shroud. Not yet.

The attendants lifted the stretcher off the ground, intending to put it inside the ambulance. Lindsey grabbed an end and wouldn't let go. "No, don't take him! Please don't take him!"

Wallace tried to unclasp her fingers, release her grip on the stretcher. "Lindsey, please. This doesn't help."

"You can't take him!"

A police detective stepped forward. "Mrs. Wallace, can I help you?"

"I have to go with him!"

"Of course, Ma'am. Just let the attendants get him . . . settled."

Lindsey looked at the detective as if he were a piece of furniture. "I don't understand," she said. Turning she grabbed Wallace's hand and squeezed. "I want Ricky. I want my baby!"

Wallace held her hand in his. There was nothing to be said. He pulled her close, buried his face in her hair, mingled his tears with hers. They climbed into the ambulance, accompanying the shrouded body of their son to the morgue.

◆ ◆ ◆

Detective Dave Chessman watched the ambulance drive away, then shook his head and went back to the task of gathering evidence. Sometimes, all you could do was keep working. His heart went out to that couple though. He'd seen all kinds of shit while working the police force, but there was nothing worse than finding the body of a child. He wanted to shout with rage. What kind of world was this? How could it happen?

He'd become a cop because he wanted to make things better, but no matter what he or anyone else did, the world didn't change. And there were always more creeps who could commit monstrous crimes like this.

"What you got there, Doyle?" he asked.

The other detective held up a pair of tweezers. In its prongs was a tiny bit of fabric. "Looks like he tore his shirt."

Chessman shook his head. "Could be anybody's shirt."

"Yeah, but it was caught on a branch almost five feet off the ground; that means it came from an adult. And look here. See how the leaves are all messed up?" He paused to take a picture of the ground.

Chessman thought of that old movie, what was it? *Butch Cassidy and the Sundance Kid.* They were trying to get away from trackers but couldn't shake them off. "Who *are* those guys?" they kept asking each other. He wished he had the talents of those guys now. That he could read the ground like a book and see the killer in action.

He sighed, took Doyle's plastic baggies of evidence and placed them in a large manila envelope. We might not be as good as those guys, he thought, but we will find the killer; no doubt about it.

"Hey Chessman, cheer up," Doyle said. "We'll get the guy."

He knew they would, but it didn't cheer him up. He might put him away for the rest of his life, but nothing would ever bring back that boy. What if something like that happened to his son? He'd find the guy if it took the rest of his life; and he'd take him apart piece by piece. Chessman frowned. Would he go that far for someone else's son? No, he thought. He was an officer of the law. He'd find him and he'd bring him before the court and watch the prosecutor take him apart.

September 7th - 7:32 AM

The Sennet kitchen was brightly lit, a frenzy of activity. Although it was only 7:45, everyone was up, getting ready for the big day. Mary could hardly contain herself. On one hand, she was grateful this day had finally arrived, and on the other, she dreaded it.

"Sit down, Peter," she said. Her son had been pacing back and forth within the small confines of the kitchen and was driving her to distraction. "Sit down. Breakfast is ready."

"I can't sit; I'm too wired."

"I know what you mean," Carl said, and Mary turned to greet her husband. She hadn't heard him come in. He didn't seem to notice her, however, just kept talking. "After all this waiting, we finally get to see that bastard get what he deserves."

"I'll be glad when it's over," Mary said as she laid the plates of eggs on the table. "This trial will be so hard. Like living through Carol's death all over again."

"I just want to see the fucker die."

"Watch your language, Peter!"

He ignored her. "Dad, when Sam's convicted, that new Eye-for-an-Eye law applies to us, right?"

Mary watched her husband think about the question and then slowly nod. A grim smile seemed etched in the stone of his face.

"And we get to choose how he dies? We get to kill him?"

Oh that was enough; she slammed the dish of toast on the table. "And you think that's good, do you? You two becoming murderers too?"

Peter only had to take two steps to get close enough to put his arms around her, and she was grateful for the strength in those arms. Funny how little babies could grow so big so fast. One day you're holding them in your arms and the next, they're so tall you get a crick in your neck looking up at them.

"It's not murder, Mom," Peter said over the top of her head. "It's vengeance. The man needs killing."

She pushed him away, and shook her finger at him. "Well, you don't need to be a killer!"

"Stop it, Mary." Carl spoke quietly, but he was the head of the house, and she had long ago buried her will in his. The habits of a lifetime strained against the words in her mouth.

"It won't bring Carol back!"

"Nothing will bring Carol back. But it will make us feel better."

Her throat felt swollen and hot, but she couldn't stop. "You think so? You really think . . . "

Carl stood up, and she involuntarily took a step back. "Look, I've killed before . . . in war . . . and no one ever deserved it like Sam-the-Slasher."

That name! That word! It ripped her control apart, and opened the doors of Hell. "Don't call him that! I told you not to . . . "

Tears, wetness, blood. Carol's blood. Oh God. When will it end? She knew that neither Carl nor Peter could stand it when she cried, but she didn't know how to stop. The vision of Carol being tortured and killed shredded her heart.

Vaguely, through the sounds of her own grief, she could hear Peter. "I just want him to suffer like he made Carol . . . like he made all of us suffer."

◆ ◆ ◆

The living room was dim, not that he cared. He'd been standing in the doorway for a while now watching Lindsey. All night, she'd been sitting on the couch, and she looked it. Exhaustion drew black circles around her eyes and lines in her face. The bright hazel of her irises, he imagined, had turned brown with suffering. Her hands kept moving, nervously pulling at a small stuffed bear. Every now and then, she'd break into sobs. John just watched, helpless to diminish her grief.

His own grief was like a tidal wave from which there was no escape. It sucked him out to sea, then picked him up and smashed him on the shore of his ruined life. Desolation and remorse drew him down and buried him in darkness.

Ricky had been a small miracle in his life, arriving long after he'd given up on the idea of ever having a son. And now there was nothing ahead but . . . bleakness and grief.

The knock on the door brought a moment's relief. It gave him something to do, a way to escape his pain. Lindsey didn't look up, so John walked through the dimness of the room and opened the door.

The daylight outside was almost surprising. He blinked.

"Sorry to disturb you so early," the man said. "I know you had a hard night . . . "

John looked the man over. He was stocky, broad, and black—actually a kind of light brown—putting him in mind of a pitbull. He thought he might have seen him last night at the crime scene, but he wasn't sure.

"I'm Detective Chessman. Can I come in?"

Awkwardly, he stepped aside and motioned for the detective to enter. Chessman stood for a moment, his eyes adjusting to the change in light. They focused momentarily on Lindsey before turning to Wallace.

"Why don't we go in the kitchen," John's voice sounded as flat and lifeless as he felt.

He made coffee. It was the first pot of coffee he'd made since . . . he found out, and it felt like he'd never made coffee before. Several times, he caught himself standing still, staring into space, having forgotten what he was doing. The policeman waited patiently while he recovered from these moments of dissassociation.

Finally, he placed two mugs on the table and sat down opposite his visitor. He took a sip. The coffee burned the roof of his mouth, a physical pain that almost felt good..

Chessman lifted the mug to his lips, and sipped politely. "I'm sorry about your boy," he said, "There're no words . . . "

Wallace grimaced, trying to shut down his imagination, the scene of Ricky's last moments that kept replaying over and over in his head. Had he tried to run? Did he fight his attacker? Did he cry? Strangling the moan that rose in his throat he struggled to focus on the detective's words.

". . . need to ask you some questions. . . . Okay? Where were you between 2:30 and 3:30 yesterday afternoon?"

Yesterday afternoon. That was a hard question. He could hardly remember anything from his life before Ricky had been . . . No. Wait a minute. It opened under him like a rapidly widening chasm—the source of his remorse. In his grief and bewilderment, he'd forgotten. For a moment, he panicked. What could he say? How could he ever explain? "I . . . was . . . at work," he answered.

The detective nodded and made a note in his little memo book. "Did anyone see you during that time?"

Wallace shook his head. Had anyone seen him? "I'm a psychologist. I see people all day long."

"But did you see anyone between 2:30 and 3:30?"

His head was exploding. "I'm sorry. I . . . I can't think . . . . I'll have to check my calendar. All right?"

The detective's face was dark and impassive, but a glint of compassion shone in his eyes. "Sure. I'm sorry about these questions . . . they're just part of my job."

John nodded.

"Anything I can do?" the policeman asked.

Wallace felt his throat swell with emotion, as he held back tears. "Just find him detective. Just find that. . . beast."

Chessman stood up and squeezed his shoulder, for comfort he supposed. Then he turned and let himself out. John clenched his hands, holding back the river of tears that threatened to pour from his eyes and drown him. He bellowed his pain and outrage to the unfeeling walls, but his eyes remained dry.

◆ ◆ ◆

Marilyn Hunter had been a defense lawyer for ten years, and Sam Reynolds had been her biggest case from the start. Even before it became the most controversial case ever to go to court. She looked over the interview once again, approving the picture of herself on the front page. Thank God she wasn't one of those "oh no, my left eye looks crooked . . . my hips are too wide" types. If she were, all this press would be unnerving.

The story left a lot to be desired though. They made her sound like a shyster. Like how could she defend someone who was obviously guilty.

The door opened and Janie walked in with a cup of coffee. She was a treasure—a secretary who didn't find it demeaning to bring the boss a little refreshment once in a while. Marilyn was grateful for that.

"So? Will this new law affect your defense?"

Marilyn frowned. "The prosecution will want to make an example of Sam. It's imperative that I get him off."

Janie set the cup down, and took a seat across from her. "Yeah. But what if he's guilty?"

Marilyn shrugged. Et tu, Brute? "Do you believe that we should all sink to the level of killers and madmen? If he's guilty he should be punished—put away for the rest of his life—not tortured."

"Tortured?!"

She leaned forward, her hands on the desk. "Carol's brother is a young man, full of righteous anger. What punishment would you choose if you were he?"

Yep. Her words had made an impression. She watched them sink into Janie's consciousness, spreading in ripples through the cage of impressions she called her self. Marilyn only hoped it would be as easy to make the jury see the danger.

◆ ◆ ◆

In his concrete cage closed with an iron door and locked with hate, Sam-the-Slasher paced. It was eight steps from one side of the cell to the other, seven steps from the back wall to the door. Since they'd placed him here fifty minutes ago, he'd taken three thousand two hundred and seventy three steps. But he hadn't gotten anywhere.

The solid metal door finally swung open, and it was all he could do to keep himself from grabbing the woman entering and beating her to a pulp. "Where the hell've you been?" he growled, his hands aching to reach around her throat.

She was her usual sassy self. "I'm not late, Sam."

Not late. Yeah, you're late, you bitch.

"Now remember, Sam," she continued, "try to stay calm. It won't look good to the jury if you get out of control."

Sam sneered. She was always ordering him around. "Hah, what're you? My mother?"

The bitch seemed unusually uptight. Good. Let her be uptight. Let her be scared shitless. Let her be any damn thing she wanted just as long as she did her job and got him off.

"Sam," she was saying in that oh-so-patient voice of hers. "You've heard about this new law?"

"You think I'm stupid? 'Course I heard."

"I'm not suggesting you're stupid. I just want you to be aware that . . . "

"You think I'm not aware? You think I don't know what's going on? You think it's easy to lead me around like the rest of the sheep? All my life people been treating me like there was somethin' wrong with my fuckin' head!"

The bitch took a deep breath. Probably countin' to ten.

"Sam let's stay on the subject! The D.A. will almost certainly call for an Eye-for-an-Eye if you're convicted. You understand?"

He couldn't help it. He pounded the table. Hurt his hand, but the way she jumped, he could see he made his point. "Oh yeah! I understand. That slimy toad, James Farrell, probably born with a silver spoon in his mouth. Lawyers! They get all the breaks and then make sure no one else gets any. Yeah, I know Farrell's gonna wanna see me fry. Well, it ain't gonna happen! It ain't fuckin' gonna happen!"

The lawyer looked smaller after his speech. He could see he'd gotten to her. He wondered if she . . . nah . . . she's too skinny to be sexy . . . all bones and muscle like a dyke or somethin' . . . none o' that fleshy softness that made women so hot . . .

"Okay," she was saying, "Let's get on with it, shall we?"

Shall we? What did she think this was? Some kinda opera or somethin'? He snorted. "Yeah baby, let's go."

◆ ◆ ◆

"Ladies and gentlemen of the jury," Judge Neely began, "You will hear testimony today in the case of the People of the State of Texas versus Samson Reynolds. Mr. Farrell, you have the floor."

He was on. This was his moment. His first chance to grab the jury and make them his. They'd been carefully picked and now everything rode on his ability to persuade. He walked slowly toward the box, making eye contact with each person. When he was close enough he placed his hands on the railing and spoke softly. His voice was calm and strong, and it sounded unrehearsed, which was exactly the effect he was trying for.

"Good morning, ladies and gentlemen. I want to thank you for being here today, for putting your own lives on a back burner while you uphold your civic duty. I know you each have other things you'd rather be doing." That got him a smile from Mrs. Pearson in the back row. He acknowledged it with a nod and continued. "This is not going to be an easy trial. You have before you a grave responsibility, a life and death decision that must be based on your perception of the truth."

A few faces looked puzzled. That was good; it meant they were listening. "Sometimes truth is hidden, and it's almost impossible to prove that a human being did or did not commit a specific act. That's why we have courts . . . and that's why we have juries." He allowed a small smile to reach his eyes.

"And that's why the law requires us only to establish truth 'beyond a reasonable doubt.' Truth . . . " He let that sink in as he walked toward the defendant's table. "Sometimes, it's hard to uncover the truth . . . . But not this time!" This was his dramatic moment; he spun on his heel and pointed at the defendant. "The District Attorney's office will have no trouble proving that Sam Reynolds tortured and killed Carol Sennet. The evidence compiled by the State of Texas establishes this far beyond a reasonable doubt."

Now he turned back toward the jury, closing the distance between them. He spoke softly. "We are not speaking here of opinions, but of facts; incontrovertible factual evidence that establishes the guilt of Sam Reynolds." He caught their eyes,

one by one, hammering it home. "Sam Reynolds is the vicious killer of Carol Sennet and we will prove it here today.
Thank you."

He was feeling pretty good as he took his seat. Let her top
that, an inner voice crowed. All eyes were on the defendant's
attorney as she got to her feet and walked toward the jury, her
heels clicking on the hardwood floor.

"Good morning, your Honor. Mr. District Attorney. Good
morning, ladies and gentlemen. I'm Marilyn Hunter, Mr. Rey-
nold's lawyer." She smiled. "I must say the District Attorney is
eloquent, isn't he?"

A few of the jurors nodded, and Marilyn nodded with
them. "But before we start calling witnesses and questioning
people, before we assign guilt, maybe we should begin at the
beginning."

Farrell gave her a point for that. Made him look like he was
rushing them toward a guilty verdict before he'd even made his
case. Smart girl.

"Sam Reynolds is accused of murdering Carol Sennet in
cold blood." She turned around and looked at Sam, acknowl-
edging her connection to him, then turned back to the jury.
"This is as serious as a crime can get, and I know you will be
careful in listening to the testimony presented before you today
and for as long as this trial lasts."

The members of the jury looked at her impassively. That
was good. If she couldn't do better, Farrell figured he'd nail
down the case easily. Although she looked good—tall, slender
and well groomed—it wouldn't be enough.

Marilyn brought her hand to her face and rubbed her eyes as
if she were tired. Nice touch, he thought. "Carol Sennet is dead.
There is nothing we can do to bring her back to life. Our responsibility today is to determine the guilt or innocence of Sam
Reynolds.

"How do we do that?" she continued. "We pay careful attention to the evidence that is offered here. Some bits of evidence will be stronger than others. Some evidence will be easy to dismiss. And some evidence will not be evidence at all, just emotional words meant to influence your decision." Here she looked directly at him, and Farrell was forced to give her another point.

She scanned the jury, stopping to look intently into each face, each pair of eyes. "You must remain alert at all times . . . because Sam Reynolds' life is in your hands." She paused for effect, drew her hand through her dark hair, waited a beat. "And he is not guilty of this terrible crime."

◆ ◆ ◆

Farrell had to admit she'd done pretty well. Two points were two more than he gave most of his opponents. Add another point for looks and the compassion in her voice, and it could be close. He watched her go back to her seat.

"Thank you, Ms. Hunter," the Judge said. "Your witness, Mr. Farrell."

◆ ◆ ◆

Only lawyers, judges, and sometimes juries enjoyed trials. Most people found them incomprehensible and dull. Justice was in the details, and lawyers were famous for nitpicking. Unlike those on TV who solved crimes in big ways, lawyers in reality usually found truth in tiny facts that had to be rooted out and separated from the coarser stuff. It was like looking for a nugget of gold in a hill of dirt and debris.

Farrell, being among those who enjoyed trials, had made the preparations and was now honing in on the gold. "Tell me, Dr. Askey, what is your specialty? What did you say you've been researching for the last twenty five years?"

"I specialize in genotyping."

Farrell didn't have to turn to see what the defense attorney was doing. He could feel her grow more tense.

" . . . in studying the DNA markers that make it possible to identify individuals." The doctor was very impressive. "You see, each individual has a unique genetic code that identifies his cells as his own. Like a fingerprint, but at a cellular level."

He went on to ask all the other questions, qualifying his expert, displaying his credentials, showing the jury how good he was. Matching the evidence with Sam's genetic fingerprint. The groundwork was laid, and now to grab the nugget. He walked past the witness stand and turned toward the jury, asking almost casually, "What's the likelihood of error, Doctor?"

"It's almost impossible that one tissue sample could match another taken from a different individual. In fact, there are mountains of evidence suggesting that DNA matching is virtually incontrovertible."

Yes! Farrell felt like dancing around the room. But just to make sure the jury got it, "What exactly do you mean by incontrovertible, Doctor?"

"I mean, sir, that DNA evidence is irrefutable, unassailable, indisputable . . . . It's as perfect a way of identifying someone as we can find."

"Thank you, Doctor," he turned and looked at Marilyn. "Your witness, Ms. Hunter."

◆ ◆ ◆

Detective Chessman looked at the meager bits of evidence on the table, and raised his head to look at Hewitt, their forensics expert. "That the best you can do? No blood? No semen? No DNA?"

"This is it. Just a scrap of fabric—looks like it comes from a cotton shirt—and a footprint we got from the ground around the boy's body. It's a size eleven Nike sneaker, almost new." Hewitt opened a drawer and pulled out a plaster cast of the foot print.

Chessman picked it up and turned it so that the light could pick out the pattern. "Not much to go on, is it?"

♦ ♦ ♦

It had been a grueling day in court, and Marilyn was tired and edgy. Walking through the barred hallways of the county jail didn't do anything to lift her spirits either. All she wanted to do was go home, have a drink, and put her feet up. Maybe turn on the boob tube and veg out for an hour or two. Sometimes mindless drivel was just what was needed to rest the mind.

She smiled at the guard—Mike Braun, the name tag said—and showed him her credentials. He led her down the corridor toward Sam's cell, and opened the door. Sam was cursing softly and looked more agitated than usual. She was relieved that the guard would be only steps away.

He was the most difficult client she'd ever had, nervous, nasty . . . sometimes he seemed just slightly mad. It might even be possible that he was guilty, probably he was guilty. No, she couldn't go there. It was her duty to defend him, and get him off if possible, and that's what she had to do.

"Sam, I think we'd better level with each other. If the prosecution wins this case, it will come under the Eye-for-an-Eye law. We discussed it earlier, remember?"

Sam snorted. "They can't convict me."

Marilyn felt her frustration showing in the lines of her face, but she had to get this said. "Why can't they convict you, Sam?"

He turned on her, like a mean, cornered animal. "'Cause they got no case!"

"Sam, just because I got that doctor to admit there's evidence against DNA testing doesn't mean that anyone believes it.

How can I argue your case, Sam? My client says he's innocent, ladies and gentlemen. He doesn't know how cells from his mouth got under Carol's fingernails? No . . . Sam, it won't work. Our best course of action is to accept the prosecutor's plea bargain—we'll plead guilty in exchange for a life sentence."

"Fuck you, Miss High and Mighty lawyer. I'm not going to plead guilty, so if you ain't on my side then get lost. Lawyers are a dime a dozen."

Marilyn drew a deep breath. "I'm trying to help you, Sam. Don't you understand? You're losing."

"You're fired! Take a hike! Get the fuck outta here!"

Well, that was just fine. Her client didn't want her anymore. Would the judge let her off the case? Not wanting to inflame Sam further, she turned and headed for the door. It wasn't going to be that easy. His big meaty hand grabbed her by the shoulder and spun her around. She ducked and was only grazed by the fist he aimed at her face. He was readying another punch, but the door of the cell swung open and that guard, Mike Braun, grabbed his arm in mid-swing.

"I don't think so, Sammy boy. Don't you know you shouldn't hit women?"

Marilyn backed up against the wall as another guard rushed in. He held the door for her, and she didn't waste any time getting out of there.

◆ ◆ ◆

"So, what do you think, Geary?" Braun said, his eyes fixed on Sam like a cat's on a mouse. "What should we do with this scumbag?"

He slapped his club against his palm, enjoying the solid thwack, thinking how good it would feel to hit Sam with it.

"Forget him, Braun; he's gonna be on death row in a coupla days."

"Fuck the both of you," Sam said.

"Ah, come on Sam, I kinda thought it was just me you wanted."

"It'll be a cold day in hell before you ever get near my ass, Braun."

Braun took a step closer and shoved the club into Sam's chest with a heavy thud. "That's Mr. Braun to you, dirtbag."

The air was heating up; he could feel the power singing in his veins. Geary pulled at his arm. "Come on, Buddy, we got other fish to fry. Let's go, Sam. Back to your cell."

Geary prodded Sam with his club, trying to herd him toward the door, but Sam didn't move. Braun pulled back on his club and shoved it into Sam's chest a second time. But Sam didn't retreat; he pushed forward, meeting the blow head on, all the time staring into Braun's eyes. After a moment, he spit on the floor, pushed past him, and allowed Geary to escort him out the door.

◆ ◆ ◆

Mike Braun strode through the corridors. The prisoners were usually verbally abusive to the guards, but not to him. When they heard his boots hitting the floor, they shut up. If they didn't, they knew he'd find a way to get them. You had to be tough with these guys; otherwise, they'd walk all over you. Some of the other guards, they called it respect, but he knew better. It wasn't respect. It was power. He had it; they didn't. And that's how he liked it.

He entered the Warden's office and waited while the secretary announced him. She motioned him in and he stepped inside, standing near the door. The Warden looked up and frowned.

"Braun, I have a report here from the prison psychologist. I've confirmed it. Seven different prisoners have accused you of excessive brutality."

Braun shook his head. "Nossir! They had it coming."

The Warden stood up. "You just don't get it do you? These prisoners are my responsibility, and you're always stepping over the line. I've seen some of the bruises, Braun."

"Oh, come on, Warden. You gonna believe me or that asshole shrink? The men are always fighting with each other."

The other man slammed his fist on the desk. "Enough! This is not the first time I've had complaints like this about you, and some of the other guards are not afraid to say what they've seen. I'm sorry, but I have to let you go."

"You can't fire me!"

"Yes, Braun, I can and I just did," the Warden stated. "And if you make trouble, then I'll have to press charges. You're out of here. If I ever see you again, it'll be on the other side of the bars."

"Fuck you!"

"Out!"

Chapter Three

September 8th - 2:38 AM

A ngela Townsend opened her eyes. For a moment she didn't know where she was. Her glasses had slipped side-sideways; she straightened them up and looked around. A gaudy red and gold oriental statue captured her attention. Mike had given it to her for their fiftieth anniversary. She'd never liked it much, but hadn't told him that, and now it had become a kind of talisman, a part of their life together. Looking at it, she always knew who she was.

The whine that accompanied the television test pattern grated on her nerves and she dug the remote out from under her and turned the TV off. Sitting up, she tried to stretch some of the aches out of her limbs, without much success. She'd been old for so long, she reflected, that she could hardly remember a time when something didn't hurt.

She picked up the dish from the coffee table and carried it into the kitchen. Washing it quickly, she laid it on the counter to drain along with the dishes and utensils from dinner. Tomorrow she'd put it all away. Not tonight.

After switching off the kitchen light, Angela shuffled through the living room and into the bedroom. The glass covered photographs that lined the top of her dresser glittered in the reflected light falling through the bathroom doorway. Idly she straightened them, smiling as she lifted the picture of her latest grandson—little Mikey—and put it down next to the one of the whole family at the beach. That had been a good day—all of them together, her boys, their wives, and all those beautiful grandchildren. Angela sighed. It was lonely being old.

Taking off her robe, she stepped into the walk-in closet and hung it on the hook that Greg had put there for her. "Hey Grandma," he'd said as he'd measured her reach. "You're such a little thing; I don't want these hooks to be too high for you."

They weren't too high, but she'd never mentioned to him how her robe dragged on the floor when she hung it up. She smiled at her little secret.

The noise of shattering glass sent her heart plummeting. Backing up into the hanging clothes, she could see a slice of the room through the partially opened doorway. Into that sliver strode a man—a big man, tall with raven hair and powerful muscles. When she was young she might have found him attractive, but now her heart drummed with fear.

In three steps he was across the room, and in a few quick motions he'd pushed all her photographs onto the floor, yanked a drawer out and dumped the contents onto the dresser. He went through her belongings quickly, tossing them aside and then pulling out the next drawer. Before Angela could get her breath he'd already ripped half her life apart.

The only weapon at hand was a broom, and she gripped it as tightly as her arthritic fingers would allow. Taking a deep breath, she stepped out into the room and took a swipe at him. "Get out of here!"

The man stepped back in that first shocking moment of confrontation. Then he started to laugh. Angela tried to hit him again, and this time the broom connected with his face. He wrenched it out of her hands and stood looking down at her.

"Get out of my house!"

The man threw the broom aside and his hand went briefly to a spot above his eye where blood trickled from a tiny cut. He held the hand in front of his face and examined the bit of red on his fingertips. Angela watched him as if she were studying a snake, not sure of what its next move would be or of how quickly it would strike.

It happened so suddenly, she had no time even to duck. His big hand came out of nowhere and backhanded her across the face, lifting her off the floor and flinging her across the room. She settled into a heap on the floor, crying now, knowing she was lost. "Go away," she begged. "I'll give you money. Just go away. Just leave me alone."

The man looked down at her and grimaced. "Oh no, mama, it's not that simple. Ever notice how things have a way of taking their course? It's like you open up a dam. It's not easy to close it."

"You can close it. You can. Just go."

In response he stepped over her and moved on to her night table. Pulling out the drawer, he found her diamond and gold wedding ring—too small now to get over the swollen joints in her hand. He smiled and looked at her. "You hit pretty hard for an old lady," he said as he pocketed the jewelry.

"I'm sorry. I was frightened. Please . . . please just go." Angela pulled herself together and tested her strength. Nothing seemed broken. She could still move.

Effortlessly, the man lifted the mattress of her king size bed and tossed it against the wall. "Me, I'm like a force of nature . . . like the wind . . . a hurricane . . . or a tidal wave. Once I'm in motion I just gotta carry on. Can you turn back the tide? Can you stop the wind?"

Angela heard the words but didn't stop to figure out what they meant. While he looked through the pouch hidden under her mattress, she lunged through the door and into the living room.

In a few quick strides he caught up with her, turned her around and hit her across the face. She felt something burst inside her cheek and blood gush into her mouth. He hit her again, sending her reeling into the wall. Sliding sideways, she found herself falling into the kitchen.

Curling up into a fetal ball, she tried, without hope, to protect herself from further harm. The young man reached down and lifted her to her feet. His hand, ever so gently, touched the blood on her lips.

"Oh mama, so much blood . . . "

His gentleness revived the hope in her heart. "Please. I can get you money. I have a safety deposit box . . . " The words sighed from her mouth; she hardly had the breath to form them.

He put his lips against her ear and whispered, "See, it's not the money. Not really."

Angela groaned. Her body collapsed beneath her. In one last wild grasp at life, she reached out to the rack of dishes on the counter and grabbed a knife. But before she could strike him, he'd taken it from her, peeling her swollen fingers off the handle one by one.

His hands found her hair and pulled her to her feet, setting the point of the knife at her throat.

"Please . . . don't hurt me . . ."

September 8th - 10:15 AM

The reporters were having a field day. The news was sensational, and everyone was watching. "No arrests have been made in the Ricky Wallace case. The police department has no leads. What a terrible tragedy."

The other anchor had some comments to add. "The interesting thing is Wallace's position as founder of S.E.E.—Stop an Eye-for-an-Eye. Now that his own son has been killed, I wonder if he'll remain as adamantly against the bill as he was before."

"That's true. After all, it's personal now."

◆ ◆ ◆

Glen Morgan IV, CEO of Titan Networks sat behind his enormous desk, watching the commentary and wondering the exact same thing. Wallace was a thorn in his side.

He watched the TV for a moment longer, then pushed one of the buttons on his desk. His assistant, Nick, ever respectful of his privacy, could now enter the office and set down the cup of coffee that he'd been holding for five minutes. And it had better be hot.

Morgan spun around in his executive chair and watched the view from his wall to wall window on New York while Nick arranged his morning snack.

"I guess Wallace won't be out waving any flags for awhile," the young man ventured.

Glen turned the chair and looked at him. "If he's smart, and I think he is, he could use this to gain an enormous advantage."

Nick looked puzzled, so Morgan explained. "His son was killed . . . he still opposes Eye-for-an-Eye. Think about it. His convictions look very, very strong."

Morgan glanced at his secretary to make sure he had his full attention. "If I don't find a way to shut him up, he could undo everything we've worked for. *Vengeance* is going to be the biggest reality thing since *Survivor*. The network stands to make billions on the TV show and spinoffs alone, never mind the movie rights. We've invested heavily in getting this bill passed, and if you think some little shit from nowheresville is going to rain on my parade, you can think again!"

He half expected applause after this impassioned speech, and Nick did look suitably impressed. Waving him off, Glen picked up the phone and began the day's intrigues.

September 8th - 1 1:38 AM

Andy woke up on a couch that was way too small for him. Sitting up, he leaned forward and picked up a roach that was all that remained of the previous night's revels. His head ached; he felt like shit and he needed it now. Too bad he didn't have nothin' stronger.

He'd laid out the takings on the coffee table the night before and now took a second look—diamond ring, gold jewelry, and cash—three hundred and thirty one dollars. Not bad for a night's work. The roach had taken the edge off, but he had to get something else and soon. Standing up, he gathered up his stuff and jammed it into his pockets.

There were no more cigarettes so he left the empty pack on the table and strode toward the front door.

◆ ◆ ◆

Sidney had trouble with his legs, but that didn't stop him from walking his dog every day. Even though it hurt, he knew they both needed the exercise. Caesar was being particularly fussy this morning and had led him out toward the middle of a grassy sward where he was finally piddling on the trunk of a big tree. The shade was welcome. That hot Texas sunshine could really get to you sometimes.

When it was all over, he'd often think how if he'd turned his head the other way he would have missed the whole thing. But he didn't. He was looking right at the door when it opened and the man came out. That wasn't right. Sid backed up into the shade of the tree and tried to be invisible.

The man stopped to pee on a bush! Sidney could hardly believe his eyes. Right there! Right in broad daylight. What a nerve! After what seemed like an eternity, he strode out the driveway, and Sid was free to investigate.

As he walked across the parking lot toward the door in question, he wondered if he mightn't be better off getting someone else to go inside, but curiosity won out. Also, who knew? Maybe he'd get to be a hero. Even if he was an old man, he could still dream, couldn't he? Despite the ache in his legs, he walked a little faster than usual. Knocking on the door, he called out, "Mrs. Townsend? Angela? It's Sid from across the way. Are you all right?"

There was no answer, so he pushed on the door, which was unlatched, and it swung open. Angela's house smelled vaguely of perfumes and deodorizers, but there was another odor on top of those that made Sid hesitate. Taking a resolute breath, he stepped into the small hallway and listened briefly, but there was no sound, only a patch of light falling through the kitchen doorway making a bright square on the wall.

Moving forward he stepped into the light. The kitchen was covered in blood, and Angela was staring . . . the look on her face . . . it would stick in his mind for the rest of his life. She was sitting on the floor, a coffee cup full of blood in her lap, her hand clumsily wrapped around the handle. Her throat gaped like a second bloody mouth, and her eyes . . . . She looked like she'd seen the gates of Hell. Sid clutched at his heart and fell backward.

SEPTEMBER 8ᵀᴴ - 1:25 PM

An icy wind blew across the graveyard, reaching into the clothing of the mourners and adding a little extra misery to their suffering. Paul Trevino watched as John Wallace drew Lindsey closer, trying to protect her from the bleakness and the cold. She didn't move away, but she didn't respond either. If you asked him, she was way too young for Wallace.

"V'yisgadahl . . . v'yiskadash . . . . The Rabbi's voice intoned the words escorting the boy into the hereafter, and Trevino briefly wondered at how different Jewish rites were from Catholic. No matter, he had a job to do.

Trevino knew Wallace well. They'd grown up together, had once been best buddies. They'd served together in 'Nam. John Wallace. He'd always thought of him as one of those ineffective do-gooders who always fucked up in the end. Officer and a gentleman. Right. Some things could never be forgiven.

The service was over, and Lindsey broke into sobs. A friend held her as Wallace watched. Poor girl. If he were her husband, he wouldn't stand by looking so helpless. He'd . . . ah shit. Never mind. Time to go to work. He maneuvered his way through the mourners and came to a stop in front of Wallace.

"John," Trevino said, "I just wanted to let you know how sorry I am."

Wallace focused bewildered eyes on the man before him. It had been years, but it didn't take long for Wallace to place him.

"Paul Trevino. Thanks. It means a lot to me to see you here. Haven't seen you since . . . well, what? '65?"

Trevino nodded, his face grim. "I just wanted to assure you that we . . . I will not rest until we find the man who did this."

Wallace looked like he was going to cry, so Trevino reached out, just as planned, and placed a bracing hand on the psychologist's shoulder. Peeking quickly at the palm of his glove and noting that he'd gotten exactly what he was after, the police chief took his leave, and Wallace turned to the next sympathetic face.

◆ ◆ ◆

The building was impressive, Chessman thought as he got out of the car and walked toward the entrance. Steel and glass. No security, he noted as he walked through the lobby to the elevator. On the third floor he got off, and proceeded down the hall to a wooden door marked, "DR. JOHN WALLACE, Ph. D., PSYCHOLOGIST."

Opening the door, he stepped inside and looked around. The waiting room was attractive, with cream colored walls and furniture. Vivid colors in the artwork and throw pillows gave the room what Chessman thought of as pizzazz. Wallace, or at least his decorator, had a good eye. Instead of the usual window in the wall, the receptionist's high, curved desk/counter was part of the room. It only took three of his big strides to reach it.

The nameplate on the counter said her name was Sally Kramer. She looked up. "Good afternoon. May I help you?"

Chessman took out his badge and showed it to her. "Yes, I'm Detective Ron Chessman, Arlington Police. I'm investigating the murder of Ricky Wallace. Do you mind if I ask you a few questions, Ms. Kramer?"

She just shrugged, so Chessman looked around pointedly and continued. "Is the office usually this deserted?"

The woman smiled. "Oh no. All Dr. Wallace's appointments have been cancelled. Except for one or two people that we couldn't reach."

"So Dr. Wallace is usually pretty busy?"

"Oh, yes indeed," she gushed. "He sees his patients here; he works part time at the prison, and I think he's involved in some other activities as well."

"What other activities?"

"Oh, you know, that S.E.E. organization for one."

Chessman made a note in his book. That was something else he'd have to check out. Maybe someone had it in for Wallace because of his work at the prison, or because of his attachment to S.E.E.. "Yeah. Well, we're working on that. In the meantime, there's always a chance that some disgruntled patient went after his son. Maybe he made someone really mad."

Sally shook her head. "Well, most of our patients are a little mad to begin with, but I can't think of anyone who could be that crazy."

"May I see his appointment book?"

He could see the indecision cross her face. Then it cleared and she handed over the book. He opened it on the countertop, flipping slowly through the pages. Wallace was a busy man. Turning to September 7th, he noted that there were no appointments between 2:00 and 4:00 when Wallace had been due at S.E.E. headquarters. That was a two hour gap at a very inopportune time. He pointed to the notation. "What was Wallace doing at 2:00?"

Sally shook her head. "I couldn't tell you that."

"Why not?"

"Well, because I go home early on Wednesdays. "

"Every Wednesday?"

"Yes. It's my afternoon off."

"Where does Wallace go?"

She shrugged. "I'm sure I don't know. I suppose he goes home."

"So you weren't here the afternoon that Ricky Wallace was killed."

"No. Why would I be?"

Why indeed. "Thank you, Ms. Kramer. I just have one more question. If you don't mind, could you tell me who closed up the office on Wednesday? Was it you or Dr. Wallace?"

"Oh, it was me. I always close up."

Chessman nodded thoughtfully as he handed back the appointment book. "Can you copy these two pages for me please?"

While she went off to do that, the detective slowly fumed. Wallace had lied to him. And he, like some newly minted rookie, had swallowed it hook, line, and sinker.

◆ ◆ ◆

The funeral had been horrible, and now because everyone had gone home at Lindsey's insistence, he had nothing to do but wander into Ricky's room and explore his loss in minute detail. He was trying to put things in boxes. But every toy, every book, every piece of clothing was imbued with memories that took his breath away. He looked at the remote controlled car in his hands and pressed it against his heart, his eyes burning with despair.

The ringing doorbell took a while to register, but eventually he came out of his pain long enough to hear it. Getting up, he went down the stairs and opened the door. Detective Chessman bulled his way in and stood there looking at, of all things, his feet.

"Nice sneakers. Nike," he commented. "New?"

Wallace was confused. "What is it? What's happened?"

Belligerently, Chessman moved in closer. "You tell me. Where were you while your son was being murdered? Between 2:30 and 3:30 Wednesday?"

"I told you. I was at my office."

"Really. Who saw you there?"

John knew that something had gone wrong, that he oughtn't to be answering these questions, but he was too tired and distraught to care. "Well, I don't know. I haven't looked in my appointment book."

Chessman's eyes sent darts into his. "You had an appointment Wednesday afternoon?"

Oh God. Wednesday afternoon . . . "I don't know. I'm not sure . . . "

Chessman held a couple sheets of paper in one hand that he now aimed at John's chest. As a weapon, they didn't have much stamina, the paper bending against his body, but Chessman kept hitting him with them anyway. "According to your office, you never have any appointments on Wednesday afternoon. So, now, you tell me. What's really going on?"

"They're not . . . always in the book," Wallace managed.

Chessman stepped back, his eyebrows raised in disbelief. "Oh. They're not always in the book. Did you see someone Wednesday at that time or not?"

Wallace backed up. He didn't want to be here, didn't want to in this room, didn't want to be in this world. "I . . . I . . . can't tell you . . . "

Chessman took a deep breath. "Listen Wallace. I'm on your side, but you better be straight with me . . . . You have no alibi."

The words came out of him in a whispered scream. "You think I killed my own son?!"

"I think you're a liar." The frown on the detective's face was cut in stone. "I don't know what else you are. Not yet." Chessman's whole body radiated disbelief and anger. "Who saw you Wednesday afternoon?"

Throwing the damning copies of his appointment log onto the carpet, Chessman turned and headed for the door, only stopping long enough to throw an injunction over his shoulder. "You stay in this house. Don't even walk outside to pick up the newspaper off the grass. You got me? The next time we meet, you better have some answers."

The door slammed. John Wallace slumped to the floor, his head in his hands. Lindsey's voice cut through air that had gone thick and hard to breathe.

"He thinks you killed Ricky?"

John looked up at his wife, and saw a stranger. "No. Of course not."

He stood up, reaching for her hand, but she yanked it away. "Why wouldn't you tell him where you were?"

A moan escaped his lips. "I don't know! I can't remember where I was!"

"You can't remember? It was two days ago! Where were you?"

"For the last time, I was in my office!"

The slap she dealt out tore into his heart like a red hot poker. "Liar! I called; you weren't there! Did you do it? Did you?"

Wallace shook his head back and forth. "I did not do it! I didn't do it!"

"Then where were you? Why are you lying to me? Oh God! Why is this happening?" Lindsey's arms hugged her body, trying to hold herself together.

John moved forward intending to offer the comfort and strength of his shoulder, but she put up a hand and held him off.

"Get away from me! I don't know what to think! I don't know what to believe! Go away!"

Horrified, hurt, and panicky, Wallace backed up, opened the front door and ran from the house.

◆ ◆ ◆

Jimmy Braddock was a happy kid, especially after school. Then he was free to do what he liked best—explore. Someday he thought he might be an astronaut. Maybe walk on the moon. Or on Mars. Wouldn't that be something? His mom said he had some imagination, and he guessed she was right. He liked to imagine things. Like right now, this old warehouse that he passed every day on his way home from school might be just any old building to someone else. But to him, it was a space station. Inside there was all kinds of stuff to play with.

Once in a while Jimmy could get someone else to come with him, but usually he liked to come here himself. Glancing up and down the street, he checked to make sure no one was watching. Then he quickly ducked through the hole in the fence, ran across the parking lot, and scrambled through the broken window that took him into the control room.

Inside, he had everything set up. He'd moved a big broken chair into the center of the room and lined up bits of old machinery around it. Taking his seat, he flipped the switch that routed all power to him. And just in time too! An enemy spaceship was bearing down on them! Take aim . . . careful now . . . Bam! They were hit! "Damage control!" he commanded. The sirens were blaring. It was now or never!

His body tensed up as he released a barrage of laser powered fireballs into the shields of the enemy cruiser. "Got ya!" he crowed.

Wait. What was that blip on the screen? "Enemy ship at 9 o'clock, Captain!" a member of his crew yelled.

"Return fire!" He spun in the chair to look at the screens behind him . . . and stopped.

Someone was watching him. Standing in the shadows behind some big crates, he was peering out at him. Jimmy could just make out a hint of white teeth. Was he laughing at him? Well, so what? "Hey, watcha doin' here?" he called out.

The man didn't answer. Just stepped out into the light. Maybe he owned the building or something. Oh wow. His mom would be really pissed if he got caught in the warehouse. She'd already told him more than once to stay away from it. Shit, he should've been more careful. "Hey, I'm sorry. If this is your buildin', I'll just leave. I didn't think it belonged to anyone. I mean. Look at it!"

The man still didn't answer, just stepped closer. Jimmy thought it was time to leave, but the broken window was behind the stranger. He'd have to pass him to get out. "I'm gonna leave now," he said and started to stroll around the perimeter of the room, aiming to get to the broken window without getting too close to the weirdo.

And he *was* a weirdo. Why didn't he answer? Even if Jimmy was wrong, he'd said sorry hadn't he? As he circled the room, he saw that the man was moving too, always keeping his body between Jimmy and the window. Feinting toward the left, the boy ran to the right and might have made it too. But the man was bigger and had longer legs. He grabbed Jimmy by the shoulder and pulled him down from the ledge he'd just managed to scramble up on.

Panicky now, Jimmy struggled in the man's grip. "Lemme go!" he cried.

The man just smiled and dragged him across the room to the center where he shoved him into the control room chair. "Play," he ordered.

Not a chance, buster, Jimmy thought, springing from the chair and careening across the room the moment the big hand released its grip. Tripping over the debris, he fell to his knees and saw out of the corner of his eye that the man was grinning. Sweat broke out all over his small body. Picking up a jagged piece of a pipe he turned, holding it out in front like a baseball bat as he slowly backed up toward the window.

The sonofabitch just watched him with that evil grin on his face. He was almost there. He could feel the sunlight warming his back. Just another step or two. Suddenly, the man was in motion, striding across the room.

Jimmy swung the pipe, aiming for the villain's head. It connected with his face, tearing a gash across it and coming away bloody. He swung again, but this time the man ducked, grabbing the pipe and yanking it from Jimmy's frightened hands.

Using the momentum, the boy turned to the window again. It was his only hope. He could see life itself written in the streaky panes of glass. Two seconds. That's all he needed.

He screamed as he was hurled from the window and thrown across the room. His back hit something hard and pointed. He screamed again and again because he couldn't scuttle across the floor fast enough to stop the juggernaut that was heading straight for him.

◆ ◆ ◆

Outside on the street, Jack Maris, Benny Wickham, and Tommy Grant were on their way into town to hang out with their buddies and tease the girls. The screams coming from the warehouse were sudden and frightening. They looked around for the source, pinpointing it just as a final scream was cut off unfinished.

"There!" yelled Tommy, pointing to the building. "In there!"

The three young men didn't hesitate; they went from zero to a full out run in nothing flat, throwing themselves at the chain link fence and running headlong across the lot to the main door. It rattled as they tried to open it.

"Let's look around back!"

♦ ♦ ♦

Inside, Jimmy was praying as he looked into the insane darkness in the eyes of the man who was holding a dagger against his heaving chest. He'd beg if he could, but the man's other hand was over his mouth. He'd run if he could, but the man was sitting on him. He thought of his mother and his sister. He remembered every word his father ever said about being smart and protecting himself. Tears leaked between his lashes and wet his cheeks. The knife . . .

♦ ♦ ♦

The man got to his feet. He'd heard the rattle of the doorknob, and knew he had to get out of there. With a last affectionate look at his latest playmate, he crossed the room, stopping only to pick up the pipe that had cut his cheek. Someone was trying to break down the side door, so he went through the window. There was a fence at the back of the property. It was high but he was tall and agile.

Quickly, he got a running start, scrambled up the concrete wall, and dropped down onto the other side. No one could see him now. He walked along the fence for a hundred yards or so, and dropped the pipe into some brambles when he heard the sirens. Straightening his clothes, and holding a hand to the streaming gash on his face, he cut diagonally across the yard of the building in back of the warehouse, and got into the car he'd parked so carefully earlier. What an adventure! Father would be proud.

❖ ❖ ❖

Tommy was the first through the door. He stopped at the sight of the boy curled up on the floor and held out his arms to stop the other boys. For a moment, it was as if time had stopped. There was nothing but that small body, the blood pooling around it, and his own breathing. Then everything was in motion again. "Check the window!" he yelled as he ran to see if the child was still alive.

"There's no one there," Jack said. "We were too late."

❖ ❖ ❖

The Property Clerk's office was pretty much deserted when Paul Trevino entered it later that night. What a day. Between the funeral and this newest child murder, he had as much energy as a dishrag. The only good thing had been that totally unexpected meeting this morning. The one that had already changed his life.

Old Randolph perked up when he entered. "Hey Randolph. Lemme see what we got on those two boys."

The clerk nodded and went over to a cabinet, pulling open a drawer and taking out two large manila envelopes: Wallace, Braddock. He brought them to Trevino and handed them over. Opening them up, Trevino looked inside, pulling out plastic baggies and arranging them on a desk.

"Don't mix 'em up, Captain," Randolph cautioned.

Paul smirked. "Now, don't go all mother hen on me, Randy. They're labeled, aren't they? Go get me a cup of coffee."

The clerk nodded. Trevino was the boss. As soon as the door shut behind him, the boss moved quickly, taking a small baggie containing a single human hair from his pocket and slipping it into the large envelope labeled "Braddock." Looking up, he saw that he was still alone. He took out the sheet of paper labeled "Contents," and replaced it with another that included the human hair. It had been easier than he'd imagined. By the time Randolph got back with the coffee, he was ready to return the whole mess to his attentive care.

CHAPTER FOUR

When John Wallace opened his living room door, the last thing he expected was to be surrounded by cops, dragged from his home, and thrown up against a police car. It happened so quickly, had been so shocking, it still hadn't quite registered. "You have the right to remain silent . . . you have the right to an attorney . . . if you cannot afford an attorney the court will appoint one for you . . . "

A part of him sat far in the distance watching the whole thing as if it were happening to someone else. He, Dr. John Wallace, was being arrested? Had the world gone mad? As they cuffed him and slung him into the back of the police cruiser like so much meat, he glanced up and saw Lindsey standing in the doorway of the house. Even in the depths of desperation, his heart went out to her. "I'll be all right!" he called out before they slammed the door. She didn't react. Just stepped back into the darkness inside the house and closed herself in.

Wallace shut his eyes and tried to block the siren out of his consciousness, but no matter what he did he couldn't block out the shame. His mind went in circles from Ricky's death to

Chessman's intrusion to Lindsey's suspicions and then to his guilty secret, and around again. And again. "You need a lawyer," a small inner voice said, tumbling him off the merry-go-round. His friend, Farrell? No, Farrell would be prosecuting.

The policemen riding in the front of the car didn't look, and wouldn't have cared anyway, as tears of wretchedness overflowed.

◆ ◆ ◆

Farrell strode forward and faced the jury. Sighing theatrically, he glanced upward as if to petition God for eloquence, then looked them in the eyes and began his closing argument. "Ladies and gentlemen of the jury, we have shown you the motive and means. You have seen the evidence—testimony that places Sam Reynolds at the scene when Carol was killed and DNA evidence that is as close to perfectly incriminating as modern technology can come.

"Sam Reynolds is guilty of this horrific crime. He brutally raped Carol Sennet. Then he cold-bloodedly flayed the skin from her breasts and thighs while she screamed in pain and begged for mercy. He is guilty. Cells from inside his mouth were found under Carol's fingernails. Can you imagine the scene? Can you see Carol struggling with this man, reaching out to scratch at the beast who held her implacably in his grasp?"

Two women in the jury had tears welling in their eyes and most of the men's jaws were tightly clenched, so Farrell knew his words were hitting their mark. The sound of sobbing from Carol's mother added just the right measure of pathos. A part of him couldn't help noting how good he was at his job.

"Can you see Carol's poor bloody hands struggling to get a grip on her murderer? Can you see her trying to rip into his face and getting only a slippery feel of the inside of his mouth? Can you feel her hopelessness and her pain as he tied her up?"

He turned away from the audience briefly, holding back the emotion. He knew he was doing well when he could make himself cry. Facing the jury once again, he continued. "Carol Sennet suffered unspeakably at the hands of Sam Reynolds. Without a speck of human decency, a shred of compassion, he raped her, then tore the skin from her breasts and watched her bleed to death . . . . This is not a man who deserves to live. This man should be put to death without regret as quickly and neatly as we would put down a rabid dog.

"But what of the others? What of Carol's brother? Her father and mother? Can the quick death of Sam Reynolds even hope to soften the pain of Carol's death? I think not, and that is why I ask that you not only pronounce him guilty as charged, but that you demand, yes demand, that he be turned over to Carol's relatives as outlined in the Eye-for-an-Eye law. Carol deserves justice. And so do they. Thank you."

Farrell knew he'd won. He could see it in the eyes of the jurors, and he could feel it in the air of the courtroom. He glanced briefly at the defense table and was disappointed yet again at seeing the court-appointed lawyer who had replaced Marilyn Hunter. He would have liked to have seen her face about now.

The courtroom resounded with cheers and applause, but even as he basked in the approval of the public, Farrell could feel the dark clouds of conscience eclipsing the sunlight of his victory.

◆ ◆ ◆

The bright light stung his eyes. It was a small room, very much like the ones you see on TV. Wallace had been in this room for hours and he was tired. He'd been tired when they brought him in; now he was a wreck.

"All right. Once again," Chessman grunted. "Tell us exactly what you did Wednesday."

"I told you! I told you already!"

The detective smirked. "That's right. Now tell us again."

Wallace rubbed his hand over his face and tried to collect his thoughts. "My first appointment was at the jail with Charles Atwood."

He'd gone through prison security and settled into his office. The door had opened and that guard, what was his name? Braun . . . had prodded Atwood in the back. Wallace could see it in his mind as if he were there. "Atwood had good reason to be angry."

"Good reason?" Chessman interrupted. He's a fucking murdering thief doing time for manslaughter!"

"Yes, I know," Wallace sighed. "But his life is a study in abuse and despair . . . Wednesday, he showed me the bruises inflicted by one of the guards . . . " They'd been black against Atwood's chestnut skin.

"Spare me this crap, Wallace! Let's cut to the chase. Where were you at 2:00? Where were you at 2:30?"

"I'm trying to tell you, Lieutenant. In the afternoon, I was at the S.E.E. office."

Violently, Chessman jumped to his feet, sending his chair crashing into the wall, and grabbing Wallace by the collar. "No, you lying sonofabitch! You haven't told us anything! Where were you when your kid was being murdered? Where'd you go yesterday afternoon when you left your house? Why do your Nike sneakers look like the print we got at the scene of Ricky's murder?"

Doyle, the other cop, the one who was playing nice and calm in counterpoint to Chessman's rage, interrupted. "Take it easy, Chessman. Go get a drink of water or something."

Glaring into Wallace's eyes, Chessman let go of his shirt and stalked out of the room, leaving him feeling as if his insides had turned to jelly. He knew it was just adrenaline shooting through his veins in response to Chessman's assault. He also knew they were playing the good cop/bad cop routine on him. But the knowledge didn't help; he was physically exhausted and that made him vulnerable.

"We're trying to make this easy for you Wallace. There's no point in not telling us where you were."

A soft moan escaped his lips. "I'm supposed to have a lawyer. I want a lawyer."

"What good's a lawyer gonna do?"

"I'm not saying another word without a lawyer."

◆ ◆ ◆

He should have demanded a lawyer from the start, but he'd thought the situation so ridiculous and trumped up, all he'd have to do was explain and he'd be on his way home. The phone they'd finally, grudgingly, allowed him to use seemed to have the oils of a thousand sweaty hands embedded in it, but he didn't care. It was a lifeline, and it was ringing.

"Marilyn Hunter."

"Hello. My name is John Wallace. Dr. John Wallace. My son was murdered three days ago and I've been arrested on suspicion . . . I need an attorney. I didn't do it."

He could hear her sighing through the line. "So they all say. You talking about the murders of those two boys?"

"Yes! They think that because I . . . "

"Don't say anything to anyone. Don't answer any questions. I'll be right there."

"I already did answer . . . "

"Okay. We'll straighten it out when I get there."

The lawyer hung up and John held out the greasy phone to the uniformed cop who was keeping him company.

◆ ◆ ◆

The Village Green was a judicial system hangout, a place where lawyers, judges, and their partners in crime could gather together after a long day and take apart the winners and losers in the great battle that consumed their lives. Today had been more significant than most, and James Farrell's name was on every tongue.

He sat at the bar getting drunk. He'd already shaken every hand in the place, and had so many drinks lined up in front of him, he'd have to come back every night for a week to consume them all. He intended, however, to down each and every shot this very night, and if he couldn't get to his feet afterward, well so be it. The world was already taking on a liquorish glow that began in his belly and spread across the lounge.

"Enough James. What are you doing?"

James lifted his head and gazed into Ginny's glittering eyes. Doing? What was he? "Drowning my sorrows."

He could see that she didn't like that; her eyes got harder and brighter.

"I don't get you at all," she said. "You won! You put a dangerous deviate away and made it possible for the family of the poor girl to . . . "

" . . . take revenge." He nodded encouragingly. Didn't she see?

"I prefer to think of it as justice."

Farrell snorted, spilling the shot he was holding. "Justish. R'venge. Whatsa diffrence whacha call it? Is still jus' state s'pported murder."

Ginny was intent on arguing with him. Dint she know it was stupid to argue with a drink? Drunk.

"Get a grip!" she was saying. "Is it murder when the country is at war? No. Is it murder when the state executes a criminal? No. It's justice."

Farrell had never noticed how close-set her eyes were. Or maybe he was seeing double? "What'd you say?"

"I *said* is it . . . "

"Oh yeah! I 'member now. All I gotta say's this: When Carol's brother gets Sam 'n tears 'm apart . . . will this be a better world?" His hands were uncannily elegant when he was drunk. He watched his index finger as it nearly poked Ginny in the eye. She brushed it away.

She was shaking her head and looked really pissed. "Oh. I get it. This is not about law, or justice, or right and wrong. This is about James Farrell! Just who do you think you are? Listen to me, James. It's bigger than you are. Straighten up and act like a man."

He tried. But when he squared his shoulders, he almost fell over. How could he straighten'p when he was drunk as a skunk? Act like a man? "So whatsa man? A killer? Does a man hafta be a killer to be a man?" He swayed sideways in the midst of his speech and bumped into her.

But she was too quick for him in this state of derangement. Before he knew what was happening, she stubbed out her cigarette and got to her feet. It was all a blur.

"I give up! Go ahead. Drown."

James might have argued, but his head was resting on the bar, and for the moment, he was unsure how to pick it up again.

◆ ◆ ◆

Marilyn stepped aside as Ginny Ormond stormed out of the bar. Her meeting with Wallace had taken just long enough to establish their relationship and make sure he would not be questioned unless she was present. Although she had enough problems of her own, she couldn't help wondering what bee was buzzing around in the assistant D.A.'s bonnet.

The Village Green was busier than usual. She took the only empty seat at the bar and waited patiently as her order was filled. Next to her, a drunken lawyer lifted his head and tried to focus on her face.

Marilyn smiled and lifted her glass. "Well, the man of the hour. What shall we drink to? Oh I know. Here's to the violent death of Sam–the–Slasher."

Farrell groaned, and Marilyn sipped her drink and studied him. "Why don't you look happy?"

His head moved slowly from side to side. "'M not happy. Not happy. Girlfrien' left me to drown 'n my mizry." Sighing heavily, he picked up another tumbler of whiskey and tried to lift it to his lips.

Marilyn didn't want to laugh but he was way off the mark, and the drink was about to be poured down his cheek. She reached out and steadied his hand. "But why are you miserable? You won, didn't you?"

"State supports murder 'n I'm s'posed to be happy?"

For a moment, Marilyn had a hard time processing what was happening. "I'm confused. Aren't you James Farrell, the D.A.? Didn't you call for an Eye-for-an-Eye today? Isn't that you on the TV?"

Farrell turned toward the television and nodded in acknowledgement. "'S me. But the law . . . the law's un . . . uncon . . . stitu . . . shn'l."

"Yeah? I know that. But I was on the defense."

" . . . Rest my case. Pass 'a bottle."

He looked like he'd already stepped over the line, maybe out over the edge, but Marilyn was not about to let this one go.

She picked up the bottle and added a few drops to an already full glass. When she looked up from her task, Farrell was studying her glassily, his index finger probing the air.

"Ya know . . . 'n law school . . . called you Ms. Bleedin' Heart. Me? Couldn' stan' you."

She smiled. "That's okay. I didn't like you either."

Farrell seemed to approve; he put his arm around her. "Hava drink, Mar'lyn. Les drown our sorrows."

Picking up the bottle, he attempted to pour it, and once again Marilyn had to steady his hand. She looked up, momentarily distracted by the television. Someone had turned up the volume.

". . . no end in sight," the reporter was saying. "Today, for the first time, a convicted murderer was sentenced not just to death, but to death at the hands of his victim's relatives. I'm talking to Peter Sennet, the brother of Carol Sennet, whose brutalized body was just two months ago. Mr. Sennet, since you may very well have the final say in the matter, how do you plan to rid the world of Sam–the–Slasher?"

The reporter pointed the mike at Peter Sennet's face. "The punishment will fit the crime," the young man replied.

A cheer went up from the crowd surrounding the reporter and the Sennets. "Do you have any specific plans yet?" the newsman asked.

"No. Not yet. But believe me, he won't suffer any less than he made Carol suffer."

A man reached up and flicked through the channels. ABC and NBC both showed marchers protesting the verdict, carrying signs calling the law unconstitutional and demanding it be rescinded. On Titan Networks a famous talk show host held up a book entitled, *An Eye-for-an-Eye: Taking Back Our Country.*" CNN was covering the international organizations that were protesting human rights violations in front of the U.N.

Marilyn said nothing, but the torrent of news was getting to her. It seemed to be getting to Farrell as well, because he got to his feet and tottered toward the door. She grabbed her purse, and followed.

◆ ◆ ◆

On the street, James pulled a set of keys out of his pocket and tried to fit one in the door of his red Corvette. Marilyn's hand closed over his. "You don't think you're driving in your condition?"

Farrell stood up straighter. ""Course not. I'm the fuckin' Distric..t 'torney. I can't drive drunk. Would be a bad . . . a bad . . . "

"Example." She guided him to the passenger side and unlocked the door.

"'Zackly. How'm I gonna get home, Mar'lyn?"

Going around to the other side, Marilyn let herself in and settled into the driver's seat. "Which way, counselor?"

Farrell had a drunken moment within his drunken moment, dizzy with the thought of this woman behind the wheel. "Straight. Go straight. But Mar'lyn, please be careful o' my car. I love my car."

Marilyn smiled at the hand he placed over his heart and put the vehicle in gear. "It's an honor, then."

◆ ◆ ◆

Despite his state, James seemed to know where he was, focusing on the road and giving directions. Marilyn was enjoying the ride when he suddenly yelled at her to stop, and tumbled out onto the side of the road. While listening to his retching, she wondered how'd she'd ended up escorting her enemy, the D.A., home.

Sighing, Marilyn got out of the car and walked around to the sidewalk where James leaned against the fender getting his breath. The neighborhood was seedy and run down, not the sort of place she'd normally go, especially at night. A liquor store just up the sidewalk was the only place still open. An appropriate place to throw up, she thought. "Are you sure this is the way, James?"

Looking up, he took in the location and her presence, and nodded. "It's a shortcut." Marilyn noted that he seemed to be standing straighter.

Suddenly, the door to the liquor store burst open, ejecting a bunch of teenage ruffians. One of them pushed Marilyn aside before crossing in front of the Corvette and escaping across the street. The shopkeeper followed, his fist raised. "Stop! You little bastards!" He stood there, impotent with rage, then turned and stomped back inside.

Marilyn wasn't sure how to react. It had happened so fast.

Farrell, now a great deal more sober, shook his head. "I see that kid every day," he said. "The youngest one. Every day he's out on the street looking for trouble. Someday, I expect to see him in court, and then I'll put him in jail."

"Unless someone does something, that's exactly what will happen."

Farrell looked at her, his eyes much clearer than they'd been all night. "Do what? What can be done? These kids are lost souls." He looked around at the darkened street. The lights from the liquor store went out. "Let's get out of here. It stinks."

She couldn't agree more. Inside the car, she turned the key and the engine roared. She wasn't finished with the conversation they'd begun. "Maybe if we tried harder . . . if the system wasn't so heartless and cruel . . . "

Farrell's lips almost smiled. "It's not cruel. It's . . . just."

Marilyn shifted into third. "Oh come on, Farrell. It's not just. It's inhuman. The more you suffer, the more you're made to suffer. When nothing is going right for you, when you can't find a way to pay your bills or keep food on the table, or get your car fixed, what happens? It breaks down on the highway, and the police come and add to your misery. You have to get your car towed or get a ticket for leaving it by the road. Everybody's got to get their cut, and nobody gives a damn whose pound of flesh they carve their living out of."

He shrugged. "That's what I'm saying. There's nothing to be done. It's way too big."

She turned the corner in the direction he pointed. "Yes, it's too big, but what if we fought it one person at a time? Maybe if kids found love and acceptance instead of hatred and violence . . . "

The red light cast a glow over car's interior, and she waited impatiently for it to change and for James to respond.

A breath of frustrated air escaped his lips. "Marilyn, if they don't get it when they're young, really young . . . I don't think they can ever get it."

"I refuse to believe that. You can't fight violence and misery by adding state supported violence and misery to the mix. You can't destroy destruction. You can only neutralize it . . . with love, education, respect . . ."

"You're still a bleeding heart," he murmured as she pulled up in front of his house.

"And proud of it. And you? What are you?"

Farrell shook his head. "Tired. I'm just tired."

CHAPTER FIVE

Wallace waited while the guard unlocked the door and led him into a small room. Although he'd been in prisons before in his capacity as psychologist, from his new perspective everything was changed. The paint was more chipped and dirty, more hopeless and ugly than before. The linoleum had scraped the grit from so many shoes, it was permanently stained. The tiny windows, recessed so high that nothing could get out and only light could get in, were entrances to a black hole. And he was inside it.

The other door opened and Marilyn Hunter stepped into the room. A beautiful woman, he noted—black hair, blue eyes, full lips . . .

She strode across the small room and held out her hand.

He shook it briefly.

"Sit down, Mr. Wallace."

John pulled out one of the chairs and sat across from her. She placed a leather briefcase on the table, and was about to open it, but instead her hands slipped off the sides of the case and came to rest on the tabletop.

She seemed to be waiting for something from him, so he blurted out the first words that came to mind. "This is crazy! I didn't kill Ricky. He was my life. I'd rather die myself than see anything happen to him."

Her face was noncommittal, but he thought that she might believe him.

"Why were you arrested?"

"I have no alibi . . . I . . . I lied about my alibi."

Tilting her head to one side, she waited for more. He didn't know what to tell her. He got up and walked over to the wall; leaned his head against it. Turning to face her, he spoke softly. "I can't say where I was."

The lawyer raised her eyebrows in disbelief. "You can't say?!" The long fingers of her hands moved suddenly, snapping open the briefcase, pulling out a sheaf of papers and holding them aloft. "Dr. Wallace, you are being held on suspicion of two counts of murder. Two boys have been killed, both at times for which you have no alibi. Your sneaker matches the footprint at the scene of your son's murder, and your DNA matches a hair found near the Braddock boy's body." She stood up, her hands gripping the edge of the table. "You can't say?"

Wallace's hands went to his face. "I'm not . . . I'm . . . Oh God! Don't you understand what this is doing to me? My son is dead. My wife hates me. And I just don't . . . want to hurt anyone."

"Who, Mr. Wallace? Who is it you don't want to hurt?"

"She has a family . . . a husband . . . children . . ."

Marilyn closed the small space between them and put a hand on his shoulder. "Listen to me, John. I can't help you if you don't trust me. You can protect this woman 'til death do you part, but understand this: Her life may undergo some . . . readjustment if you expose her, but you may lose yours if you don't."

He held back the tears that threatened. "I'm such an ass-hole."

Marilyn nodded. "Most of us are."

"I don't even love her. I love my wife . . . . Even if . . . she admits she was with me, who will believe her now?"

Sighing, the lawyer crossed her arms in front of her body and looked up briefly before focusing her intense blue gaze on him. "It's harder now. You've lied to the police. You've lied to your wife. People won't be inclined to trust you, but if she admits she was with you, you're one step closer to freedom."

"I need to think."

"You have to help me help you, John."

She seemed to be waiting for him to respond, but he couldn't think of anything else to say. Picking up her papers, she laid them back in the briefcase and snapped it shut. Then she walked away, stopping to say one last thing before she knocked on the door. "When you decide whether you want to live or not, call me."

The door opened. The lawyer exited. The guard came for him. John Wallace, swallowed by a black hole, walked back to his cell blinded by the tears that had finally broken through the dikes of his self control.

◆ ◆ ◆

In a different jailhouse, Sam Reynolds entered another little room, this one even more squalid than the last. Paul Grant stood up when the prisoner entered, and extended a hand in greeting. Sam stared at the hand and spit on the floor. Grant let his arm fall to his side.

"I'm Paul Grant," he said. "From the ACLU. Here to help you with your appeal." Sam didn't react. "You are going to appeal, aren't you?"

The prisoner sauntered over to the table and leaned against it. "Why? Do you think I'm guilty too?"

"Mr. Reynolds, I'm not here to judge you one way or the other. I'm only here to help you file the papers that will overturn this decision. You do plan to appeal?"

Sam tamped a cigarette against the back of his left hand. "I plan whatever I plan, and no law says I gotta tell you my plans."

Grant shook his head, puzzled by the sudden shifts in the conversation. "Whew . . . I seem to have gotten off on the wrong foot. I'm on your side. The Eye-for-an-Eye law is unconstitutional and we want to bring this case before a higher court where it can be . . ."

"I knew it was unconstitutional!" Sam crowed. "You think I'm stupid, don't you? Just 'cause you been to college, you think the rest of us are ignorant and stupid. Well, I knew that law was unconstitutional before you walked in here." Stepping forward, he poked the attorney in the chest. "So you can take your expensive suit, and your leather briefcase, and your college education and get the hell outta here!"

Grant stepped backward. "Reynolds, I'm here to help you!"

"You trying to help yourself! Don't think I don't know it. All that publicity . . . it's like a drug to you lawyers. Well, you ain't gonna hitch a ride on my wagon, Bud, so get outta here before I get mad!"

"You're in serious danger, don't you understand?" There's a time limit on appeals. If you don't file the papers, you could die!"

Sam moved in even closer, his face up against Grant's. "Don't threaten me, ya little shit! I take on bigger men than you in my sleep!"

Grant took another step backward. "Sam, you're being just a little irrational . . . I'm not threa . . ."

Suddenly, Sam's meaty hand held his lapels. He pushed Grant up against the wall. "And I been called bigger names . . . now get this: I hate lawyers and I hate you!"

The door to the room opened and a guard called out for reinforcements. In a few moments, the room was filled with guards and Sam was on the floor. Grant straightened his suit, took a deep breath and exited. As he took a final look at Sam Rey nolds, a phrase came to mind: "terminal stupidity."

◆ ◆ ◆

Andy's apartment was a shithole. That's why he didn't bother to clean it. Hell, he couldn't remember the last time he'd taken out the trash. The dirt didn't bother him much though. All he really cared about was having a place to crash and a nice little stove.

Stumbling out of the bathroom, he pushed past a pile of junk and old clothes in the hall, and stepped into the kitchen. A coupla dead cockroaches lay belly up on the counter, and a coupla live ones went scurrying into dark corners.

The stove was grimy, but that din't matter. He lit the gas and started cooking up his freebase. When the white powder had turned into a yellowy paste, he mashed it into a pipe and lit it up. The first hit was the best, and the second was even better.

He was flying, and the knock at the door barely registered. Until it came again.

Carefully, soundlessly, he moved toward the door and peered through the peephole. The two blue uniforms sent his belly plummeting through his shoes. The pounding on the door was becoming more insistent. Flattening himself against the wall, Andy quickly considered his options. They were slim: fight or flight?

He could take them. He was bigger and meaner. And he was high. So high he could fly. Like lightning he moved down the hall to the bedroom and started digging through the piles of stolen goods and old clothes littering the room. Every beat of the cop's stick on the front door sent an electric chill up his spine. Where was it? Where the fuck did he put it?

Finally, his hand closed around the cool metal of the gun, and he extracted it from the mess. Suddenly the room was organized. Funny how a gun could do that. Where all was disorder and chaos, a gun was so solid it drew every eye toward it. It was like gravity.

Pulling out the clip, he saw that it was fully loaded and ready to go. Just like him. The pounding at the front door came to a stop, and Andy froze. He heard the lock groan when the cop's foot hit it. It was a flimsy lock. Wouldn't stand up to this kind of assault for long.

Taking a few deep breaths, he positioned himself beside the door. The next kick splintered the wood, and the one after that shoved the door open. Andy waited breathlessly. When the man in blue stepped through, he squeezed the trigger and watched as if in slow motion as the red flower bloomed, tearing through the blue sleeve and splattering Andy's doorframe. He'd been aiming for the neck, but oh well, at least he'd hit him. The violence would give him a little time while the pair of uniformed assholes regrouped. He could hear one of them shouting into his radio for backup.

Turning, Andy flew back to the bedroom and shut the door, hoping the second cop wasn't planning to be a hero. The bullet that ripped through the wood and planted itself in the opposite wall was answer enough. Without aiming, he shot wildly and careened into the bathroom. The window was small, but he might be able to flee through it. Lucky he was on the first floor.

Without wasting a moment, he broke the glass with the gun and went out head first. Sirens screamed down the street. If he didn't get away now, it would all be over. Scrambling to his feet, he slid along the wall at the back of the building. Which way? His head said go over the fence, but his feet said go into the next yard.

Andy could hear the cars screeching to a halt and footsteps pounding the pavement as cops took their positions. He peered around the side of the building and pulled his head back in time for the bullet to miss. Shit, he was in a mess. Try the fence. He could be across the yard and over the chainlink in less than a minute. Shooting the gun as he ran, hoping to hit someone, or at least provide himself with some cover, he soon emptied the clip and threw the useless weapon on the ground.

The cops closed in like vultures, and in moments, he was on the ground being kicked and beaten. Then he was hauled to his feet, handcuffed, and thrown into the back of a squad car. Worst of all, the high was wearing off, and he would soon be stone cold sober.

◆ ◆ ◆

Through her kitchen window, Virginia Copeland had a good view of the trash cans in her neighbor's side yard. She picked up her coffee mug and took a sip, turning the pages of her magazine absently. Normally, she'd be interested in finding out how to tell if a man is the right one for you, but today she was just bored. Her fingers picked a cigarette out of the pack of Marlboros on the table and brought it to her lips. Now, I'm a chain smoker, she thought, as she used the remains of her last cigarette to light it. She turned another page. Boring, boring, boring. She'd prefer to be at work.

A movement outside caught her eye and she glanced up. Impulsively, she patted her hair and headed toward the side door, stopping only long enough to check her reflection in the glass.

Her neighbor was stuffing a sack of garbage into one of the cans. "Hi Mr. Stokes. How's it going?" He was an attractive man, and she'd been trying to catch his eye for some time. He looked up and Virginia gasped. "Wow! What happened to your cheek?"

Stokes put his hand to his cheek, and smiled ruefully. "It's nothing. I was cleaning out my garage three or four days ago and this mean mother of a pair of hedge clippers jumped right out at my face. Laid my cheek wide open."

Virginia looked closer and touched his face gently, the nurse in her assessing the wound. "You're lucky you didn't lose your eye."

Stokes nodded. "You got that right . . ."

His green eyes were fixed on hers and for a moment she caught her breath. At last, something to get involved in . . .

The scream from in front of the house interrupted the line of force connecting them, and Virginia turned to see her eight year old daughter, Amy, wheeling her bike around the corner of the house. Her face was streaked with tears.

"Mommy! Look what Sean did to my bike! On purpose!"

The tension in Virginia's body had been building all day and had finally found a potential outlet, and now this! "Not now, Amy. Put the bike away, and I'll look at it later."

"But he broke it on purpose!"

God, what was she going to do with that boy? She looked past Amy to where Sean stood on the sidewalk in front of the house watching them. The last thing she wanted to do was get into a fight with Sean now when she'd finally gotten a chance to talk to Bill. Glancing at him, she smiled apologetically.

"You meanyhead!" Amy yelled, "I hate you! I hope you die!"

"Amy!"

Sean's reply was to raise his middle finger to his sister. Virginia felt her cheeks flush. She wanted to say something to Bill, but had no idea how to recapture the moment.

Stokes was generous about it. "Ah, you know brothers and sisters . . . always fighting." He winked at Sean who glared at him and strode off. Then he knelt down and looked at Amy's bike. "It's nothing, just the chain come off." He smiled at Amy. "You want me to fix it?"

Amy nodded, brushing the tears away, and Virginia felt a wave of gratitude sweep over her as she watched Bill flip the bike over and get to work. Momentarily, the world was a little brighter. She put her arm around her daughter and they shared a smile.

◆ ◆ ◆

Her sister held her hand, turning it over, brushing it against her cheek as if it were fur. Sometimes, it was scary the way Charlotte fixated on her hands. Ginny gently pulled it away, and then used it to lift Charlotte's chin. "Hey. Hey, Charlotte."

Her sister's eyes would never make contact with hers. Instead they roamed all over the room, over the nurse's station, the television screen, the patients playing cards, the bars on the windows. No matter how many times she visited her here, it always broke her heart.

Ginny dropped her hand into her own lap, and watched Charlotte drop out of this world. She'd seen it happen so many times. It was like a switch clicked. Charlotte's eyes no longer looked out; instead they looked inward. Sighing, Ginny stood up. "I have to go."

At first Charlotte didn't respond and Ginny thought she was home free, but then her sister wrapped her arms around her and wouldn't let go. "Don't leave!"

There was no extricating herself from Charlotte now, so she just held her closer, whispering over and over. "It's all right. It's all right Charlie. Don't worry, I love you. Shhh."

And Charlotte cried. "Don't leave me here. Don't leave me!"

"You're safe here, baby. And I'll be back soon."

"No! I'm not safe! I saw a man looking through the window!"

"No one will hurt you, honey. Look, there's no one out there."

"I wanna go home, Ginny! Take me home."

Ginny held her closer and tried to hold back the tears. "Soon, Charlie. Soon, we'll be together. Please believe me. I will take you home. Soon."

Helplessly, she waited until the nurse strode toward them, pried Charlotte's arms apart and held her so that Ginny could leave.

"Sorry, Ms. Ormond. Come on Charlotte, your sister has to go now."

"No! Stay! Stay!"

As she walked away, Charlie's voice crying out behind her, Ginny could hardly see for the tears in her eyes.

Chapter Six

In court, no such feelings intruded. Ginny Ormond, Assistant D.A. was a legal machine with no other desire than to see criminals punished and justice served. She had nothing but contempt for the scum who stood before the court trying to save their pathetic hides from the iron hand of the law.

She glanced briefly at the defendant, then stood up as Judge Walters entered the court.

The judge took her seat and motioned them all to sit. Her sharp-eyed glance fell on the prosecutor. "Ms. Ormond. Good morning."

"Good morning, Your Honor."

The judge turned to the defendant standing alone at the defense table. "Mr. Ridley, you understand that this is not your trial. This is an arraignment. Do you know what that is?"

"No ma'am."

Ginny thought the man quite handsome. Most of the degenerates passing through the courts looked the part. But this guy looked like a fucking movie star.

"Today, you will enter a plea of guilty or not guilty. If you say that you are not guilty, we will then set a date for a trial before a jury. If you say that you are guilty, we will set a date for sentencing."

"Oh, I'm guilty," Andy Ridley stated.

Ginny looked at the judge, wondering what she'd make of that.

"Mr. Ridley, do you know your rights?"

"Yes, your Honor."

"Why are you not represented by counsel?"

"I need a lawyer to plead guilty?"

The judge frowned and sat up straighter. "You've been charged with first degree homicide, Mr. Ridley, a capital crime."

"Your Honor, I just want to get this over with. I'm guilty. I killed the old lady as sure as shit . . . I mean . . . I did it. She was as defenseless as a rabbit, but I killed her . . . "

Ginny was shocked, and judging by the rise in decibels, so was everyone else in the courtroom. In all her years as a lawyer, she'd never seen two cases go down the same way, but this was one for the books, why wasn't he pleading insanity? Was the guy totally nuts?

Judge Walters banged her gavel. "Mr. Ridley, you have the right to remain silent. You . . . "

"She was in my way . . . She was ugly . . . I don't know. Somebody or something's been pullin' my strings all my life . . . ."

If he was planning an insanity plea, this was a really stupid way to go about it. Ginny looked at the judge, who seemed to be momentarily speechless. The courtroom waited in silence.

"I see, Mr. Ridley. Does the prosecution have anything to add?"

Ginny got to her feet. "Your Honor, the District Attorney's office would like it made clear to the defendant that if he pleads guilty we will prosecute to the full extent of the law."

"You'll call for the death penalty?"

"Your Honor, we will call for an Eye-for-an-Eye."

The Judge turned toward the defendant. "Do you understand this, Mr. Ridley?"

The man nodded. "Yeah, I understand. The old lady's relatives get to have a go at me."

The judge shook her head. "Doesn't this frighten you?"

"What's the difference. I'm gonna die anyway. Yeah, it scares me; you think I'm made of stone? But I don't have no say in the matter, anymore, do I? I did it. I killed the old bitch. Shot that cop too. And to tell the truth, I enjoyed it."

◆ ◆ ◆

Wallace stepped into the small room with its beat-up old table and chairs and breathed a sigh of relief as the guard left, shutting him in. He'd hated the walk through the prison hallways, the gauntlet of catcalls and hostile thrusts. "Hey Doc, a little different on the inside, ain't it?"

Yes, it was different. He was torn apart. He wanted to die. Wanted to live. Wanted to confess. Wanted to cover himself in lies. He wanted to run; to stop running. To scream in frustration and anger. He hated with all his heart as much as he'd once loved.

His foot tapped impatiently on the dirty linoleum. The scene that was brewing would not be pleasant, and the sooner it was over, the better.

The door opened, and Marilyn Hunter stepped inside. Behind her was Lindsey. He didn't know whether to look his wife in the eye or hide his head in shame.

Marilyn left them alone in the room, but he barely noted her departure. Lindsey, looking frail and bereft, stood there, her eyes searching his face.

"Oh Lindsey . . . I'm so sorry."

His words touched her; a tear slipped down her cheek and he could see that it was difficult for her to hold back the flood.

"No, John, I'm sorry. For a moment, when they arrested you, I thought . . . that you . . . that you might have . . . . I was out of my mind with . . .

His hand lifted, almost of its own accord, and he placed his finger against her lips. Such tenderness welled in him as he had never known. "Shhh . . . it's not your fault. It's mine."

Lindsey moved into his arms, and laid her cheek against his shoulder. He could feel the rhythm of her heart in her temple where it pressed against the coarse prison shirt.

"You loved Ricky as much as I did," she said.

"Yes, I did." He held her away from him so that she could see his eyes. "Promise me you'll never stop believing that."

Pain was palpable between them, and they rallied against it in the only way they knew, holding onto each other for life. Wallace knew he had to say what had to be said and silently prayed that this tiny raft of security would not be blown apart by his words.

"Lindsey," he whispered to the top of her head," there's something I have to tell you . . . it's hard . . . Lindsey, I love you. I guess I never realized how much until now . . . I was so full of myself, you know? I thought my success was due to my own superiority, and I forgot all the people who made it possible. Especially you.

"It's all right, John. We're together now."

Wallace took a deep breath and sighed. "No, it's not all right. You were there for me when I needed you . . . helped me build my practice, helped me develop my reputation. You gave me a son . . . Oh God, I've been such a shit!"

Like a wall, it came between them: doubt, suspicion, fear. Lindsey backed away. "What did you do, John?"

"It didn't mean anything to me . . . I swear to you, it's you I love!"

He watched the wall grow solid as the light dawned in her eyes.

"Who is she?"

"She's no one. It was just a fling." He stepped toward her but again she retreated.

"That's where you were the day that . . ."

Couldn't she see how this was killing him? Reluctantly, he nodded, and fell back devastated, as his wife turned and rushed to the door of the room, and started banging on it.

"Let me out of here! Open the door!"

"Lindsey! Please! Forgive me!"

But she was gone, and all that was left in the world at this moment were the pitying eyes of Marilyn Hunter as the guard stepped in and escorted him through the gauntlet back to his cell. This time, he heard nothing.

♦ ♦ ♦

Mary Sennet's darkened living room felt like a prison cell. No, actually it was her heart that was behind bars. She cried softly, trying not to disturb her husband or her son with her unwelcome emotions. But despite her efforts, Peter apparently had heard her. He came down the stairs.

"Mom, are you all right?"

Pulling herself together took great effort, but she managed a weak smile and wiped the tears from her face. Peter wasn't buying it. He sat down next to her on the couch and put an arm around her shoulder. Tenderness was the last straw. She burst into sobs.

"Mom. Mom, it'll be okay."

Mary held onto her son and cried into his shirt in despair. "Oh Peter, I'm so confused. Carol was murdered, and I'm filled with hate for the man who did it! I lost my child and because of my hate I also lost God. I haven't been to mass since the funeral. I don't understand what's happening to us. You and your father will have your revenge, murder the murderer, and then what?"

"Oh Christ, Mom, it's not murder!"

"Will it bring us peace? Will Carol come back to us? Will all the nightmares and horror go away? Will God return?"

Peter pulled away from her. "Stop it! Just stop it!"

But she couldn't stop; there was more to say, and like it or not, he had to hear it. "I'm afraid, Peter. I'm afraid I'll lose you all—Carol, you, Carl—I need to forgive. But how?"

Peter stood up, looking at her as if she were a stranger. "Some things can never be forgiven."

◆ ◆ ◆

Judge Ryan Neely looked up as Carl and Peter Sennet were escorted into the inner sanctum of his private chamber. "Come in, Mr. Sennet. Please sit down."

The two men, old and young, but not so dissimilar otherwise, took seats facing him.

"As you are aware, this is very informal. The punishment of Sam Reynolds is, according to the law, entirely up to you. Whether I agree with this or not is immaterial. My only function at this point is to review your plan and make sure the State of Texas can accommodate you."

Peter Sennet drew some papers out of his breast pocket and opened them up on the desk. Neely began to read, feeling the blood drain from his face as he took in the details.

Peter smiled. "It fits the crime, wouldn't you say?"

CHAPTER SEVEN

OCTOBER 8ᵀᴴ – 6:15 PM

On Death Row, forgiveness was no longer an issue. Sam-the-Slasher Reynolds lay in his bunk staring at the ceiling. In his hands was an official letter that the guard had handed him not long ago.

The slot in the door opened and the guard passed a tray inside. Sam could feel his eyes on him, but he didn't look up. "What's for lunch?" he growled.

"Oh, the usual: filet mignon, lobster . . . "

Throwing his legs over the edge of the bunk, Sam snorted derisively, and stood up. He took the tray and set it down on a small table.

Sitting on the bunk, he grabbed the hamburger and tore a piece out of it with his teeth. "Yep. It's delicious. Just what the condemned ordered."

"What you talking about, Sam?" the guard asked. "This ain't your last meal."

"Might as well be." He picked up the letter. "You know what I got here? This letter is from the Governor's office. It says that because I didn't file no appeal, 'the execution will go forth as scheduled.'" He could hear his voice, how it sounded normal even when mouthing these hateful words.

The guard frowned. "Yeah? I been wondering about that, Sam. Why didn't you file?"

The muscles in Sam's face tightened. "Hell, that law is unconstitutional." He could almost feel a great void opening up beneath him.

"Well, maybe so, but you gotta file."

Falling! He was falling!

Jumping to his feet, he nearly knocked the table over. "Fuck them! Fuck all those slimy suits with their books and their fucking laws. I want them all to die! You too, you stupid ox! Get the fuck away from here!"

Shaking his head, the guard stepped forward. "You know what, Sam? You're in there, and I'm out here. So who's the stupid one?"

Now he saw nothing, heard nothing, only the rush of blood in his ears and the red rage that filled the world. Grabbing his lunch tray, he threw it at the bars of the cell as the guard walked away laughing. Shit, now he'd have to eat his lunch off the fuckin' floor. Fucking moron . . .

Outside the prison gates, a protest had been going on all day while Sam picked french fries off the concrete, took a nap and dreamed of hell, then woke to a splendid last dinner with the warden as witness. The minutes ticked on.

◆ ◆ ◆

Jack Decker and others from S.E.E. held lighted candles and carried signs demanding the repeal of the Eye-for-an-Eye law. At twelve midnight, just a few hours from now, if S.E.E. couldn't stop it, Sam Reynolds would be murdered, and the government would call it legal. He just couldn't allow that. It was wrong. It was just plain wrong. He was a veteran and loved his country. This law, he believed, would destroy everything America stood for.

His sign read, "An Eye for an Eye Makes the Whole World Blind." He also liked some of the others: "Stop this CRIMINAL law!" "Eye-for-an-Eye is UNCONSTITUTIONAL!"

Decker's small group of protestors walked slowly back and forth in the road in front of the prison gate. Although it was supposed to be a peaceful demonstration, there were others out there on the other side of the road who seemed to feel as strongly as he did that the law was okay. That it made *justice* possible, not legalized murder. Decker couldn't understand that. But he did understand the undercurrents of emotion that were fueling the crowd.

The two groups had been heckling each other across the road for most of the day, and tempers were getting more and more frayed as the night wore on.

Eyeing the opposition, Decker noted that their so-called leader, Mike Braun, was striding toward him. He'd heard about that bastard from Dr. Wallace. Braun had been a prison guard who took every opportunity to beat up those in his power. And now that he'd been fired (or so Decker had heard on the grapevine) he seemed to be more rabid than ever in his support of Eye-for-an-Eye.

A commotion inside the gates captured Decker's attention. Several guards stepped outside and started herding the protesters out of the way. "Back! Move back! Get out of the road!"

There wasn't really anywhere to go because there were fences on both sides, so as the guards pushed the two groups back, they also pushed them toward each other.

Decker saw that Braun was standing just a few feet away and was looking right at him.

"They're gonna bring out that slasher creep now! I hope they fry his brains!"

"Yeah, you'd probably like to watch," Decker yelled back.

"Damn right! I'll be glued to my TV!" Braun moved forward aggressively, but Decker stood his ground.

"Why? Does it get you off?"

The ex-prison guard lunged, taking a swing at him that he barely evaded. He was going to take him on, but a couple of Braun's buddies grabbed the man's arms and held him back. "Asshole," shouted Braun.

"Fuck you!" Decker returned.

As Braun struggled against the arms restraining him, a police van came through the gate and moved down the drive.

"It's Sam!" someone yelled. "They've got Sam in there!"

At that, both groups began running after the van, but it soon disappeared from sight. Nothing to do then but stand there impotently watching as the hated supporters of that murderous law cheered and jeered their triumph.

October 9ᵀᴴ – 11:59 PM

Farrell had no choice but to be part of the solemn group that had been appointed to witness the death of Sam Reynolds. He sat next to Trevino watching as the news crew checked their sound levels and set the lenses of their cameras against the one-way glass. The execution would be broadcast nationwide on Titan Networks, the reality show to end all reality shows. The official spin was that it gave the audience the chance to see that justice was done. Farrell would have put it differently.

As the door inside the little room they were viewing opened, Trevino smiled. "Let the games begin . . . "

No one cared to comment.

◆　◆　◆

Peter and Carl Sennet followed the four guards leading Sam into the room. His hands were handcuffed behind his back, and Peter could see the white outlines of his flesh where it pulled against the metal. Standing to the side with his father, he watched as the four guards attempted to immobilize Carol's murderer.

As the first guard bent to chain Sam to the leg irons attached to the concrete floor, Sam kicked him in the face. Throwing his body against the second guard and knocking him down, he successfully turned and thrust his knee into the groin of the third.

Peter could hear the collective scream from the viewing room as Sam, unimpeded, ran toward the one-way glass, his head down like a battering ram. He moved forward, but the fourth guard beat him to it, tackling Sam from behind and bringing him to his knees. Peter smiled. He could just imagine the sigh of relief as the spectators tittered softly at themselves and moved back toward their seats, all the while keeping their eyes on the struggle between Sam and the guards.

One guard had a bloody nose where Sam had kicked him, and he was rough as he and the others wrestled their prisoner into place and held him there while they snapped the leg irons around his ankles. Once he had been effectively bolted to the floor, the guards visibly relaxed and stepped back.

"Big men! Fuck all of you!" Sam shouted, still struggling.

No one responded. Instead the guard with the bloody nose grasped one of the manacles hanging from the ceiling and with a little help from the others, snapped it around Sam's flailing right wrist.

Another guard then removed Sam's handcuffs and his left wrist was forced into the other hanging manacle. The chains were tightened and then Sam could no longer move.

"Bye Sam," the guard muttered through the blood still dripping from his nose.

Sam spat at him as he and the others turned to leave.

Peter had a knife in his hand and he rolled it back and forth between his fingers as he circled his prey, thinking about Carol and how she had been treated by this monster. He liked the feel of the knife. The impotent rage that had filled him for these last months had at last broken free. Retribution would be his.

"Come out so I can see ya, you pussy!" Sam yelled.

Peter had no intention of doing anything he didn't want to do. Not anymore. He moved closer to Sam, breathing in the stench of his fear, and laid the point of his knife against the back of his neck.

"Go 'head! Go on! Do it!"

Peter grabbed Sam's shirt and sliced through it from the neck to the hem at the bottom. Then he sliced through the sleeves, and if he nicked the bastard a few times, so what. It was just a precursor to what was to come.

◆ ◆ ◆

Andy Ridley lay back, his hands under his head. He felt weird, as if his mind and his body were in two separate places. It was a little scary; maybe he did have a soul. If he did, would it go to hell when he died? Ah, he didn't believe in all that crap. Dead was dead. And this life had become too painful to live. No coke, no grass, not even a drink to take away the pain. Better to be dead.

All his life, he'd never had a break. He'd watched his mother die when he was two and she hit a truck. He'd seen her head come off. Then he'd been thrown from the car and broke just about every bone in his body. Through all the next year as he cried and grieved, all he could feel was the guilt of knowing that he'd survived. All he ever wanted in all his life was to go back and stop that truck. But all he ever encountered was anger and hatred. His father said it was his fault . . . no . . . no use thinking about that. And then the women—all those women—wanting just one thing. He'd learned to hate them too.

He'd been working on a little poem to keep his mind busy. It wasn't much, but he'd scratched it into the wall with a piece of broken plaster and now he read it to himself over and over: Tomorrow we die, don't have to fry. Tomorrow we die, don't have to fry. Stop saying that shit, that ain't it. Tomorrow we die, can't tell no lie. It's late. It's late. I'm full of hate. Can't stop what's coming down. Why wait? It's fate. Got a date with Fate. She loves her bloody clown . . . "

◆ ◆ ◆

Judge Bertram Neely sat back in his leather recliner and took a sip of his scotch. He was sure he was going to need some fortification against the television show he was about to watch, but given that he'd been the judge presiding at Reynolds's trial, he felt it was his duty to see it through.

He took another sip, and picked up the remote. Maybe it was time to retire. The show, *Vengeance*, the very idea of it, made him nauseous. What was happening to this country? After this, what next? What about that Ridley character? He was crazy. There was no doubt about it. And given that Ginny Ormond, as acting D.A. was prepared to go for blood, Neely was hesitant to let Ridley go without a trial. A good attorney could probably get him off on insanity. On the other hand, the man was guilty. Guilty as sin. Guilty as the devil himself. Why fight for such a worthless life? Neely moaned softly, gulped the last of his drink, and aimed the remote at the television screen.

◆ ◆ ◆

Moving around in front of Sam, Peter Sennet ripped the shirt off him, exposing his bare chest.

"We're going to do the same to you that you did to my sister."

"Yeah? You gonna rape me? What you gonna use? That little pencil dick you got?

Peter smiled. He had thought about that. About using a broomstick maybe, but as much as he might have enjoyed it, he didn't think it would work on television. "No, we're just gonna cut you like you cut my sister."

"Yeah, I cut your sister. And she screamed her guts out, so come on! Come on! Go ahead, cut me!"

Peter raised the knife and slid it against Sam's trembling flesh. No blood came. It wasn't as easy as he'd thought even with the image of Carol vividly burned into his imagination.

"Come on, you gutless wonder! Kill me! I raped your sister! I stuck it in her, and she loved it!

◆ ◆ ◆

Inside the Rodeo Bar and Grill, the patrons were going wild. The televised execution brought out more noise and emotion than the World Series and Superbowl combined. Here was the real thing, and every eye was on the big screen TV. A disclaimer ran continuously at the bottom of the screen saying, "This material is unsuitable for children. Parental discretion is advised." Above that Sam-the-Slasher was screaming, "Yeah man, she loved it! That's why I cut her! The dirty whore liked it!"

Carl Sennet came up behind the raving prisoner and belted him across the side of his head. "You fucking liar!"

Peter glanced at this father. "He's just trying to make us so mad that we'll kill him fast. But you can forget it, Sam," he continued as he slid his gaze back to his victim. "It's not gonna work. It's gonna be slow . . . very slow . . . and very painful."

Even on the screen, the viewers could see that Peter's cold-blooded assessment had had an effect on the prisoner. His eyes widened just a bit. Then Peter angled the knife just a bit and sliced it into Sam's chest. A red line appeared in its wake.

The crowd cheered. This was the best reality TV they'd ever seen.

Sam grimaced and tried again. "You know what your sister liked best, buddy boy? She really liked it when I put it in her mou . . . " Carl Sennet's second blow cut him off.

Carl hit Sam again and again, but Peter grabbed him arms and shoved him backward. "Dad, if you knock him senseless, he won't feel anything! This isn't what we planned!"

"All right! Do it then! Just do it!"

Peter picked up the knife and sliced down, cutting off a piece of skin. Sam screamed.

"Come on, you piece of shit, tell me again what you did to my sister!"

"I didn't! I didn't!" Sam pleaded.

Peter raised the knife again and sliced off the nipple.

"Fuck, oh fuck!"

"Come on shithead, where's your big mouth now?"

"Peter," Carl yelled, "End it! This is wrong!"

"No way," his son replied, "I'm just getting started! This is what he did to Carol!"

As the intensity of Sam's torture increased, the mood in the bar began to turn ugly. "Turn that shit off!" someone shouted.

♦ ♦ ♦

Inside the viewing room, Farrell could see that the cameraman was visibly shaking. Bending over, he took a couple deep breaths. One of the other witnesses got up and left and Farrell could hear him in the hall retching. Even Trevino was looking sick to his stomach.

"I'm not going to stay," he said to the captain.

"Hell, it's just beginning," Trevino said.

Farrell shook his head. "I'll see you tomorrow."

"Yeah, well this will probably go on for hours. I'll probably sleep in tomorrow."

Farrell had seen enough. He stood up to leave, noting that he wasn't the only one.

♦ ♦ ♦

Sam was a mass of quivering bloody flesh. The room was soaked in blood and bits of meat as was Peter Sennet. It was sticky and unpleasant, and he was tired. But he was far from done. Turning, he noted that his father was huddled in the corner of the room, the lines of his face etched in horror. Well, it couldn't be helped. Someone had to do it. And if his father wouldn't, then it had to be him. The skin on Sam's torso was pretty much gone, so Peter began the finale by cutting away his pants.

♦ ♦ ♦

In a darkened living room, another witness, Bill Stokes, smiled and sipped his beer. What a show! It should get an academy award.

♦ ♦ ♦

Glen Morgan smiled at the battery of TV monitors. What a show! And the cost of production was next to nothing—no special effects, no high priced actors. Nothing but profits. Pure profits. He was a genius.

CHAPTER EIGHT

OCTOBER 10ᵗ́ʰ - 10:24 AM

F arrell was sitting in Paul Trevino's office drinking coffee
and eyeing the crack in the glass of the open door when he
heard the unmistakable sounds of his friend making his way
through the outer room toward his private domain.

A chair shoved back and a raspy voice: "Mornin' Captain!
Some mess last night, huh?"

"You never saw such a thing in your life. Blood everywhere . . . the poor father crying . . . the brother . . . jeez!"
That was Trevino. Footsteps. He was getting closer.

"I know, sir. I saw it on TV."

"Yep. Sam-the-Slasher slashed to ribbons."

Another deeper voice rumbled, "An Eye-for-an-Eye . . . a
life for a life . . .

"Justice."

Trevino's face appeared in the doorway, and Farrell
couldn't help frowning at how chipper he looked. He was wearing his usual suspenders with his badge pinned to them, and
looked as if he'd slept the sleep of the innocent.

Trevino wasn't surprised to see him there. "Well, if it isn't the weak stomach himself."

"Did you enjoy yourself?" Farrell asked.

"Not as much as I did afterward . . . "

A faint leer momentarily crossed the captain's face. What was that all about? Farrell wondered.

"No Farrell," Trevino continued, "I didn't enjoy myself. But I saw it through because it was right. It was just. And after what they did to that slasher, scum like that will think twice before they cut up any more innocents."

Farrell snorted, "That's a crock. Killers act on impulse, and they don't stop to think about consequences. The death penalty has made no difference whatsoever in the rate of violent crime."

Trevino pulled his chair out and settled into it. "Yeah? Well wait and see what the statistics show when killers realize they can die like Sam."

Jumping to his feet, Farrell put his hands on the desk and leaned forward belligerently. "Come on, Paul! Look at this Ridley we're holding. He admits he killed a defenseless old lady in cold blood. But the guy has been so strung out for so long, I doubt he remembers his name half the time much less the fact that he'd die a horrible death if he got caught. Don't you get it? Didn't you see what happened to the Sennets? Do you think Peter Sennet is a better man for having become a murderous . . . "

"He did what was right."

Farrell threw up his hands and sat back down. "He did what was wrong. How can you not see that? His father was crying, begging him to end it."

"What the hell do you want from me?!"

The older man's face was getting red, and there wasn't any point to this anyway. "Nothing! Nothing. Listen, I'm taking a leave of absence, so cancel our breakfasts for the next few weeks."

Now Trevino was on his feet. "Over this? You're walking away from your job over this?"

Farrell didn't know whether to nod or shake his head. All he knew was that he couldn't send another man to a death like Sam's. "Yeah, over this."

Pushing aside the remains of his breakfast, he stood up, took a last look at the captain's shocked face, and walked out.

As he hurried across the breezeway and into the building where his own office was located, Farrell tried to get a handle on his emotions. He was angry, upset, lost, confused. He wanted to scream, to cry. His entire body felt like it was being pulled in a million different directions. He didn't know what to do, only that he had to do something.

Entering his office, he noted that there wasn't really that much to be done. Throwing things into a box didn't take long. He was only interrupted once when Janet came in asking about the paperwork on the water tower the city was trying to condemn. Turn it over to Ginny, he'd told her. He'd already spoken to the assistant D.A., and she was thrilled at the opportunity to take over his job for as long as he wanted. She didn't understand or care what he was going through. That was obvious.

OCTOBER 13ᵀᴴ – 2:58 PM

Bill Stokes sat on his porch drinking a beer. It had been a quiet day. The bushes separating his house from that of his neighbors rustled briefly, and then that little girl from next door skipped out from between them. Stokes smiled.

"Hi there. How's the bike?"

"Did you see my cat, Angel? She's missing."

Stokes smiled more widely. He loved this game. "What does she look like?"

The child appeared to be thinking. Did children think? "Well, she's pretty. She has grey fur with stripes and little white feet." This last came in a breathless rush.

Stokes took his time answering, as if he were pondering all the cats he'd seen in the last few days. "Is the fur in her ears white? And does she have white fur on her chest?"

The girl clapped her hands and jumped up and down. Oh please. "Yes! That's her! Have you seen her?"

Stokes shook his head ruefully. "You won't believe this (*if you had any sense*), but I found a cat just like that the other day. I thought she was lost, so I gave her food. She's inside. Probably sleeping . . . "

"But she's *my* cat!" She was actually wringing her hands!

Bill patted her head. "Oh, don't worry. You can have her. I was just taking care of her 'til her real owner came looking for her."

Even her blonde curls seemed to relax at that. "Can you give her back to me please?"

"Sure," Stokes replied and stood up. "I'll just go find her." Opening the back door and leaving it open, he went into the house, moving slowly through each room. After a few minutes he stepped back through the door. She was still standing there. "I can't find her. When I do, I"ll bring her over to your house, okay?" Turning, he pretended he was going to go back inside.

"Wait! Why don't you call her?"

"Huh? How do I do that?"

A big grin lit up her face. "Silly. You don't know how to call a cat? You go like this: Pss . . . Pss . . . Pss . . . "

Stokes watched as the child went through the door and into the kitchen, then followed behind her. Once inside, he quietly closed the door and bolted it.

CHAPTER NINE

OCTOBER 13ᵀᴴ – 5:41 PM

Virginia was tired. Come to think of it, she was always tired. What with work, shopping, cooking, cleaning, laundry, driving the kids here and there and all the rest of the joys of single-motherhood, she had precious little time to do any of the things that gave her pleasure. She was always rushing from here to there and back again, and now that she thought about it, she wasn't just tired; she was exhausted.

She pulled the car into the driveway and opened the door, lifting out the bag of groceries she'd picked up on the way home. Now to do dinner. Then clean up, then help Amy with her homework, and then finally, after a workday that began at 6 am and ended at bedtime, she could sleep.

The key turned in the lock and she carried the food to the kitchen. It was late. Where was Amy? And where was Sean? Not that she'd expected him to watch his little sister. Oh no, that would be too much to ask of the selfish little SOB.

Virginia grimaced. Never in all her life did she imagine that she would ever think of her own son in such terms. This was not how she'd planned it. Her mother had been a good mother, and she would have been even better. But then she was left on her own with two babies and no support. And what could you do? You did your best.

Walking across the hall to the small bedroom that belonged to Sean, she pushed on the big "Do Not Enter on Pain of Death!!" sign, and walked in. What a mess. Did all kids think of the floor as extra closet space? The only place that wasn't cluttered was the ceiling.

Maybe Sean was like his father. He was angry about Dan's leaving, that much was certain. But it seemed to his mother that he was also angry about everything else.

Shaking her head—it was pretty hopeless—she turned and went up the stairs to the tiny upstairs bedroom that was Amy's. It was nearly 6:00. Where was her little girl?

"Amy!" she called.

After checking out the back door and calling all of Amy's friends' mothers, Virginia was really beginning to worry. She hurried out the front door and, getting into her car, drove up and down the block calling. "Amy!" God, when she found that girl, she'd kill her herself. Amy knew she was supposed to get off the bus, go home, and stay there unless she had permission to go elsewhere.

Where the hell was she? It was almost dark. Pulling back into the driveway, she jumped out of the car and was about to go inside. Then she wondered if her neighbors knew anything. Next door on the right, the house was dark. The Petries weren't home yet, but she could try the other one. His living room lights were on.

Chewing her nails, Virginia waited on the porch of Bill Stokes' house, observing that the peeling paint around the windows fit right into the neighborhood. The door opened at last.

"Mr. Stokes, I'm sorry to bother you, but have you seen Amy today?"

Stokes looked concerned. "No, ma'am. Is something the matter?"

"Oh no. I'm sure it's nothing. She's usually so dependable though. I just don't get it."

Stokes nodded understandingly. "Well, you know kids . . . They just follow their impulses . . ."

A tear crept down Virginia's cheek. Where was her little girl? Embarrassed, she turned awkwardly and fairly leapt off the porch.

♦ ♦ ♦

The basement was dark and shadowy, and Amy Copeland lay curled up in the musty corner, her arms tied behind her back. Ropes bound her ankles and wrists together, so that if she moved, the bindings either wrenched her shoulders or her thighs. She was immobile; a thick band of duct tape covered her mouth. Her pretty kitty, her little Angel, lay in a heap of dead fur just inches from her tear-wet face. The stench was awful. There was nothing in Amy's mind but a black well of pain and terror, Angel's empty eyes, her mother's arms . . .

♦ ♦ ♦

At 7:15, the police knocked on the door and took Virginia's report. By now she had been reduced to frantic, near hysteria. She wanted to scream, to bang her head on the wall, to throw herself under the wheels of one of the trucks rumbling by the next street over. Amy. Amy. Amy.

"When did you last see her, Ma'am?"

Virginia hugged herself tightly. "This morning when she and Sean left for school. She's supposed to get off the bus, and be here when I get home. She's only alone two hours . . . "

"Do you think she's with her brother?"

Oh sure, that's why I'm disintegrating here, 'cause she might be with her brother . . . . "No. If I thought she was with her brother, I wouldn't have called you."

"When will her brother be home?"

"What does her brother have to do with this? Why aren't you out looking for Amy?"

"Ma'am, I'm trying to help you." His tone of voice made it sound like a threat. Like, answer my questions, or I'm gonna drop the whole thing.

"I know. I'm sorry," Virginia tried to be softer. "He'll be home late."

"We'll want to talk to him."

"Please, find my daughter. This isn't about my son."

◆ ◆ ◆

The bars of his cell made patterns on the walls. Wallace studied them as if they were Rorschach blots, as if there might be a clue in the shadows that would make all this comprehensible. A late news program blared from the guard's radio at the end of the hall, going on and on about him. Him. How the hell had this ever happened to him?

"According to Captain Paul Trevino, the missing girl, Amy Copeland, has nothing to do with the two boys who were brutally murdered in early September. Trevino is satisfied that the killer of those boys, John Wallace, is safely behind bars. More on Wallace and his murdered son when . . . "

"Guard!" Wallace yelled. "Guard!"

"Shut up!"

"I need to talk to my lawyer!"

"Sure. Tomorrow."

Wallace wanted to grab the guard by the neck and slam him into the bars of the cage. He'd seen it done in the movies so often. He'd even seen the guards do that to prisoners in real life. Yeah, but it wouldn't work for him. Quelling the inner violence threatening to tear him apart, he forced his voice to sound calm and conciliating. "Please. I go to court tomorrow. I need to talk to her now. Didn't you hear? That kid who was kidnapped?"

"That make you happy, wise guy?"

Wallace gritted his teeth. The worst of it was the unthinking hostility everywhere you looked. He could hear the chair scraping the floor as the guard got up. "No, of course it doesn't make me happy, " he said. "But don't you see? It proves that I . . . "

The footsteps were getting louder. "It don't prove nothing," the guard said.

"But the killer might have unfinished business with girls too! Don't you . . . "

The guard strode into view and stopped just outside his cell. Wallace stepped back involuntarily at the absolute menace he projected. Suddenly, the other noises in the jail became more pronounced: the sullen laughter, the angry hoots, the nasty comments.

The guard moved closer, spitting his words. "Shut up. I heard enough from you."

Wallace stared into those intimidating, unreceptive eyes for just a moment before turning away. He sat down on his bunk. Closed his eyes. If only he could sleep.

Chapter Ten

Marilyn had arrived at the courthouse a little early, so she sat in her car, sipping her coffee. On a whim, she opened up her cell phone and tapped out a number. She knew she probably shouldn't do this, but she was doing it anyway.

A secretary answered. "District Attorney's Office."

"Is Mr. Farrell in?"

"No, I'm sorry. Mr. Farrell is on a leave of absence. Do you want to talk to Ms. Ormond?"

Now, what was that all about? Marilyn wondered as she dialed the number he'd given her the other night.

Pick up, she thought. Pick up. "James? Hi. It's Marilyn Hunter. I'm sorry to call you at home, but my curiosity got the better of me. Why aren't you at work?"

James laughed, but it sounded bitter. "I guess I'm not as tough as I thought I was. Did you see what they did to Sam-the-Slasher?"

"No. I couldn't watch that."

"Yeah, well, it turns out that neither could I. I also couldn't continue as DA if I would have to see that done to anyone else. So here I am."

"Wow." That sounded dumb, but Marilyn honestly couldn't think of anything to say that wouldn't. "Do you want to talk about it?"

She could almost see Farrell's eyes narrow as he thought about it. "Actually, I would. Do you?"

Smiling now, she couldn't keep the lightness out of her tone. "I'd love to talk to you about it. Other things too."

"Hmm. A mystery. How 'bout tonight?"

"Perfect. I'll see you then." Marilyn snapped the phone closed and smiled.

◆ ◆ ◆

Wallace paced the small holding cell waiting for his lawyer, waiting for the trial to begin, waiting for this all to be over. Finally, the door opened admitting Marilyn Hunter.

"Did you hear about that girl?" he cried. "They don't think it could be the same killer because it's a girl, but that's not so! I'm a psychologist. I could tell you a dozen reasons why a killer could switch from boys to girls!"

Marilyn held out a suit on a hanger. "Better calm down and get dressed, John. You look like you haven't slept in a week."

Wallace sighed. "I haven't. But don't you see? If they find the real killer, they let me go."

"John, I'll see what I can do. In the meantime, we have to go to court, so go change your clothes. Wash your face and compose yourself. Okay?" There was no response, so she gently shook his arm. "Okay?"

It took some effort, but he pulled himself together and took the suit from her. The guard who had been waiting outside escorted him down the hall.

◆ ◆ ◆

While he was getting dressed, Marilyn went over her notes for the trial. Her case was weak and she knew it. All she really had was John Wallace himself, his history, his altruism. But would it be enough? The door opened and Wallace re-entered. Marilyn looked him over. Shaved, dressed, and cleaned up, he looked good, and the shadows of grief and pain in his eyes only added to his appeal. He'd make a good witness in his own defense.

◆ ◆ ◆

Farrell had been sitting around in his underwear contemplating the wreckage of his life when Marilyn Hunter's call woke him from his lethargy. What was the point of this leave of absence if he wasn't going to use it to do some good? Enough moping around.

So here he was sitting in his Corvette watching the street for someone who might have some of the answers. His red car was pretty conspicuous in this neighborhood, but no one seemed to have noticed just yet. The street corner looked like it did every day when he went past on his way to work. He wasn't quite sure why he was here, just that if there was any buzz out on the street about the murder of those boys, he might be able to dig it up.

That kid was there again, the one he and Marilyn had talked about the night Sam was convicted. What a shame. He looked like a nice kid, except that he was smoking, hanging out on street corners, and doing God-knows-what-else with his older buddies.

A police car cruised down the street, and Farrell watched as the kid and his gang disappeared before the cops reached the corner. After they'd gone, the boys reappeared. Quite a talent, Farrell thought. Why were they hiding?

Getting out of the car, he crossed the street and confronted the five boys. The four bigger ones stared at him as he spoke to the kid. "I'd like to talk to you, if you don't mind."

"I do mind," the boy retorted. "Who the hell are you?"

"My name is James Farrell. I'm trying to find out who murdered those two boys."

"Hey Sean," one of the big boys hooted. "Do he think it's you?"

All the boys laughed at that, but not the kid, not Sean. "Oh, now you guys think I had something to do with that too! I don't know nothing."

"Yeah, he don't know nothing."

"I didn't do nothing," Sean continued. "Some fucking pervert kidnaps my little sister and all of a sudden the cops are all over my ass."

"Your sister?" Whoa, Farrell thought. Back up. Who is this kid? It didn't look like he was going to find out, as the five boys were already starting to walk away. Farrell made a grab for Sean's arm. "Wait a minute!"

The boy shook him off, but he did stop. The other boys ambled on down the street.

"I'm not a cop," Farrell insisted. "And I don't think you had anything to do with these murders or with your sister's kidnapping. Your sister is . . . Amy Copeland, right?"

"I don't give a shit who you are. Just fuck off and leave me alone."

No, no, Farrell shook his head. It was not going to go down like that. "There's a man in jail who may die, horribly, for something he didn't do. I'm just trying to find out the truth."

The scorn in Sean's eyes said it all. "Oh sure. I bet you got that hot little Corvette by caring about the truth."

That hurt. Farrell sighed. "I thought I did. I did. The trouble is sometimes life opens your eyes to truths you wish you didn't have to face. You know what I mean? It's like your sister disappears and suddenly life isn't about hanging out and having a good time anymore."

"What do you know about it?"

Farrell heard Sean's friends hollering for him to come on, but for some reason, the boy was still listening. He had to make every word count. "You know, yesterday I was the District Attorney. I was important, making big money. But today, I'm just a man trying to decide what matters and what doesn't. Haven't you ever felt like that?"

"Yeah. Yesterday, I was the son of a single mother with no time to look at me. And today, my sister's missing. Now, it's like I don't even exist . . . except to the cops."

"Do you have any idea what might have happened to your sister? Have you noticed any strange guys hanging around the school yard? Do you have any suspicions? Any ideas at all?"

Too much. Too fast. He could see Sean's mask harden into place.

"I told you. I don't know nothing. And if I did, I fucking wouldn't tell you."

With that, the boy strode off to meet his friends across the street. Farrell cringed as Sean spit on his Corvette.

◆ ◆ ◆

Trevino's office door was open, and Farrell walked in uninvited. The captain looked up from the computer and swiveled his chair to face him. Farrell winked, set a paper bag down on the desk, and handed the older man a container of coffee. Trevino opened the bag and unwrapped a bagel while Farrell sat down opposite him. "You hear about the missing kid?" he said between bites.

Farrell nodded. His own bagel was suddenly dry and tasteless, and he put it down on the desk. "What the hell you doing here anyway? Why aren't you out looking for her? You can't just sit around and wait until you have another body on your hands."

Trevino narrowed his eyes, but his response was non-committal. "We don't have much to go on."

"Have you talked to the neighbors?"

"Of course we talked to the neighbors. That's what we do. Come on Farrell, what's with you?"

Farrell sighed. "This whole thing is just getting out of hand. Do you think she was kidnapped by the same freak who killed the boys?"

"No, I don't." Trevino was rummaging through his top drawer. Finally, pulling out an old toothpick, he continued. "Look at the facts: Wallace killed boys. Wallace left bodies hanging around. This is someone else. M.O. is different."

"Yeah, but maybe he's just treating her different because she's a girl."

Trevino's laugh was almost a bark and his tone was sarcastic. "Oh sure, and maybe he'll take her out dancing before he cuts her. No, Farrell, this is another man."

Farrell sat back in the chair. "Well, I think you should be out looking for him instead of sitting here stuffing your face with bagels and cream cheese."

The toothpick seemed to be stuck between Trevino's teeth. He dug around some more and finally removed it. "Bossy, aren't you?"

"Yeah, it's a fatal flaw."

Now it was the captain's turn to sigh. "Thought our breakfasts were cancelled."

Farrell looked at the clock, which read 11:29. "It's not breakfast. It's brunch. And I still say it's the same guy."

Leaning forward, Trevino's face was deadly serious. "Listen carefully, Farrell; I'm not going to repeat it. Two boys. Two bodies. Lots of blood. All we have is one missing girl, zero bodies. No blood. It doesn't compute."

"Your blood arithmetic never ceases to amaze me. The only thing wrong with it is that I know Wallace; I saw him a few hours after his son was murdered. He couldn't have done it. It had to be someone else!"

"Yeah? Well, I know Wallace too. Shit, we grew up together."

"So you know what I mean! He's not. . . "

Trevino stood up, his posture aggressive. "Hey! Idealists can be just as dangerous as anyone else. . . . I should know. Look, we have DNA evidence that places Wallace at the second murder. What more do you need?"

Farrell almost wanted to back off; the chief was so adamant, but he said nothing.

The captain looked at his watch. "Shit," he said, his tone once more pleasant. "The luncheon. You coming? Lots of pretty girls there . . . "

Farrell nodded. "I'll just finish my coffee." He watched as his old friend patted his pocket to make sure he had his wallet, and pushed his chair under the desk.

"Okay, I'll see you there. Lock the door behind you."

After Trevino left, Farrell sat for a moment sipping his coffee. Then he got up and walked around to the other side of the desk. The computer was still on, and he sat down to pull up the files on the missing boys and print out everything the police had on Wallace so far.

◆ ◆ ◆

The luncheon was one of those self-aggrandizing rites where everyone in the loop is given special awards for being in the loop. Farrell couldn't even remember the name of the quasi-political organization sponsoring the event until he saw it strung over the dais. "Citizens Against Violence," the sign announced.

As he approached his seat next to Trevino, the diners were applauding the opening remarks made by the president of the organization. He pulled out the chair reserved for him and sat down.

"Thought you weren't going to make it," the chief remarked.

Farrell shrugged.

The president was almost finished. "And now, I'd like to introduce our illustrious police captain, Paul Trevino."

Farrell had always enjoyed the captain's speeches. The man had presence. His stocky frame seemed to inflate, becoming larger and more imposing. Yet he had a down-home quality that brought in the votes.

"Thank you, Mr. President, Ladies and Gentlemen. It's my pleasure to be here today. Truth is I can never turn down a free meal . . . "

It was an old joke, but it always worked. The audience laughed appreciatively.

"We're here today to give our stamp of approval to the Eye-for-an-Eye law and to celebrate the end to the reign of terror in this state."

He was preaching to the choir and predictably they applauded loudly at that.

"With this new law, violent crime will be drastically . . . "

Farrell knocked over his glass of water, and jumped up. Truth be told, he didn't really know what possessed him. He just couldn't seem to help it. In the background he could still hear Trevino, but he knew the audience was watching him.

" . . . reduced. We can expect our streets to be safer; our children to be freer. What more can we ask of a society than that it provide us with safety and freedom?"

The crowd loved it.

"Just one week ago, Sam-the-Slasher, a vicious murderer, was executed, not by the State of Texas, but by those . . . "

Farrell finished mopping up the water and took a drink from what was left in the glass. It sent him into a coughing fit, which he tried to discreetly contain. Everyone in the audience looked at him, but Trevino continued.

" . . . who suffered the most, the father and brother of Carol Sennet, Sam's victim. Some say that the penalty was more vicious than the crime, but I say it . . . was . . . just."

They were on their feet now loudly declaring their approval.

"Tonight, Andrew Ridley, who savagely murdered a helpless 78 year-old woman will get what he deserves. An Eye-for-an-Eye is a deterrent that will work where the death penalty never did. When criminals see that murderers die swiftly, surely, and painfully, they will think twice before committing their atrocities on innocent victims."

The applause was deafening, and no one clapped louder than Farrell.

◆ ◆ ◆

Trevino didn't speak to him all through lunch, and Farrell didn't really blame him. He just hadn't been able to help himself. The whole thing was taking on a life of its own. In fact, he hardly knew himself anymore. No one spoke to him, so he sat with his glass in his hand watching the diners as they ate, drank and mingled. From the dais he had a clear view of most of the room.

Suddenly he sat up a little straighter. Wasn't that Ginny? God, she was beautiful. He wondered if she was still mad at him. She probably was, but after all: nothing ventured, nothing gained. He got up to go and see. Keeping his eyes on her, he strode through the crowd, coming to a sudden stop when he saw Glen Morgan, CEO of Titan Networks, appear at her elbow. She greeted him as if they knew each other. So, was that it, he wondered? Was she messing around with someone bigger, richer, and more powerful?

Morgan put his arm around Ginny and led her through the double doors at the entrance to the room. James followed discreetly, watching from just inside behind one of the doors. He just couldn't help himself. She had certainly been quick to replace him. Morgan turned to survey the empty reception area, and James ducked out of sight. After a moment he peeked around the edge of the door in time to see Morgan reaching inside his jacket, producing a small rectangular package and passing it to Ginny. As she dropped it into her capacious purse, Farrell's suspicions abruptly took another tack. He froze, not knowing if he'd seen what he'd seen, as Morgan turned and walked away. Farrell had just decided to follow Ginny, when someone clapped him hard on the back, almost knocking him off balance. When he'd recovered, she was gone.

◆　◆　◆

Leaving the building, Farrell and Trevino were thrown together by the movement of the crowd. By this time, the food and drinks had mellowed Trevino's temper, and Farrell thought it was probably a good time to apologize. "Sorry about your speech," he began.

Trevino threw an arm around the younger man's shoulders. "Farrell, you s.o.b., don't tell me you're sorry. I know it was deliberate, and if you weren't like a son to me, I'd . . . "

"Come on, Chief. Would I do that to you? I know how much you love the limelight."

There was no more time for talk, however; the reporters were upon them. Someone stuck a microphone in Trevino's face. "Captain Trevino! How is Ridley going to die?"

"Isn't it true that Carl Sennet is undergoing psychiatric care?" a voice called out.

"What did you think of the execution of Sam-the-Slasher?"

The crowd of reporters dogged their heels as they walked down the stairs and headed for the larger crowd on the sidewalk. Pickets were being held high and Farrell could feel the tension in the air.

There were two groups facing each other. On one side were the picket signs reading "An Eye-for-an-Eye is legalized slaughter!" "Stop Eye-for-an-Eye: S.E.E." Farrell recognized some of the people from Wallace's organization. He was glad to see that they were there. On the other side he thought he recognized a guard he'd seen at the prison. The man pushed through the crowd, his picket held high. "Go get 'em Trevino," it read.

"This'll stop 'em," someone cried.

◆ ◆ ◆

"Hey! I have an idea," Drew Townsend said. "Let's use clubs. You know, beat the sonofabitch to death."

Gary frowned. "Way too messy."

"Yeah, and too . . . ." Robbie's voice trailed off. He was the youngest of Angela Townsend's grandsons, and the least inclined to violence.

"Too what? Too mean?" Drew leaned forward aggressively. "Too cruel? He killed our Grandma, Robbie!"

"I know!"

"Look, we want him dead." Gary had a way of seeing to the heart of things. "He doesn't deserve to breathe the same air as the rest of us. But do we have to become animals just 'cause he's one?"

Drew looked at Gary in admiration. "Now there's an idea."

"Huh?" Robbie said.

♦ ♦ ♦

"All in all, it's been a hell of a day." Farrell sighed and took another sip of his drink. Marilyn had let him talk until he felt as if he were talked out. He looked at her interested and interesting face and smiled. "I'm not usually so self-centered. Want to tell me what your day was like?"

She chuckled softly and smiled back. "Well, I went to court with Wallace. The trial's just begun . . . "

"He didn't do it."

Marilyn lifted her drink. "How do you know?"

"I told you." Farrell said, "I know him. Either I'm completely wrong about people and have no judgment whatsoever or he's innocent."

"I think so too. But that DNA evidence! What the hell am I supposed to do about that?"

Farrell picked up her hand where it lay on the table and held it lightly. "The only answer is to find the real killer. Then all the rest will fall into place." Suddenly, he was acutely aware of Marilyn's hand.

"Well, you can count on me to help in any way I can." Her eyes met his and in them he could see that she too was moved by the touch of his hand on hers. Gently, he brought her fingertips to his lips, never letting go of her eyes.

Her breath caught. "Oh James," she said, "I know I shouldn't say this, but it feels like coming home." Her hand moved silkily from his lips to his cheek, unfolded, turned and caressed the line of his jaw before pulling back and resting once more on the table.

It was all getting away from him. In these last days he felt as if his life were unraveling quicker than he could weave it back together. Now this. How could he do this when everything was in such turmoil?

Marilyn sat up straighter; to him it looked as if she were gathering herself back into herself. He did the same, but he knew that something world-shattering had just happened. "Let's find the killer. Then we'll have time to figure this out."

She nodded and lifted her wineglass. James watched the light glinting on her lips, her eyes, and the dark waves of her hair. He wondered why it had taken him so long to see beyond her lawyerly exterior to the soft womanly glow shining from within.

CHAPTER ELEVEN

OCTOBER 15ᵀᴴ – 12:06 AM

I t was a little room, made out of concrete. Andrew Ridley was led by his guards into the room as three young men followed closely behind.

"Too late, too late . . . can't hold back fate, can't stop what's going down . . . " Andy recited. He was glad it was over, and he didn't struggle as the guards snapped on the leg irons and hand-cuffed him to the chains hanging from the ceiling. He didn't wonder what was in the two wooden boxes that were on the floor next to the door.

One of the guards whirled his index finger around next to his ear. "He's loony tunes," he said. The other guard shook his head and the two of them left Andy there . . . alone with the three young men who were to be the instruments of his fate. Robert, Drew and Gary had all loved their grandmother, Angela Townsend.

◆ ◆ ◆

Inside the viewing room, the appointed group of witnesses awaited the execution, some reluctantly, some with relish. The

air was heavy with pent up emotion, and Ginny Ormond imagined she could feel it pressing down on her. On the other side of
the one way glass, one of the young avengers advanced on
Ridley, reaching out and tearing off his shirt. Ginny, seated in
the front row, had anticipated this; her lips parted. What a body!
What a waste!

A knife came out and slit through Ridley's pants, down one
side and up the other. Ginny leaned forward, although the view
couldn't get any better. As the final cut was made, the pants fell
away, and she gasped, as did others in the viewing room.

On the stage that was the little room, the three men froze for
a fraction of a second.

Time seemed to stand still. Gazing at Ridley's spectacularly
under-endowed genitalia, Ginny almost understood the forces
that had brought him to this place on this day. For just a moment, his great lack juxtaposed with his physical beauty dented
the walls she had built to protect herself, and she almost felt the
psychic pain that had made him what he was.

The moment passed.

"What are they doing?" Ginny whispered.

Next to her, Trevino shrugged. "Beats me."

The cameraman made adjustments to the equipment to better capture the reflection of light on Andrew Ridley's body.

Through the window, Ginny saw that a bucket had been
produced, and the men were painting Ridley's naked skin with
something that looked like lacquer. She watched his face as they
painted it. His mouth opened slightly and an inquisitive pink
tongue tasted the substance.

"Sweet?" she heard over the loudspeakers.

"Yeah, it's sweet," Drew said. "Wanna know why?"

Andy did not respond. Angela's grandsons then went out of
the little room and shut the door. Ginny looked at Trevino.
"This is getting really weird." Then one of the wooden boxes by

the door jumped and fell over, and a tiny yellow and black bee crawled out, testing the air. Ginny cringed as it was immediately followed by a swarm. The buzz of the bees filled the room and the air behind the glass was black with them.

"No!" Andy screamed as the stings forced him out of his self-induced lethargy. In moments he was covered with a living blanket of bees, and was writhing in pain.

"Oh, this is sick shit," Trevino muttered.

"What's the matter?" Ginny grimaced. "You bothered by a few bugs?"

Inside the viewing room the air was stifling, and people's breath came short and fast as they listened to the endless screams of the condemned. Eventually, Andy's voice lost its volume and became a whimper. Then it stopped.

He hung limply from his manacles as the bees began to leave his body, flying back into the wooden box with the load of honey they'd ingested. Drew, Robbie, and Gary stepped into the room wearing protective clothing and used a smoker to drive the remaining insects into the box.

After removing their masks and gloves, they went over to Andrew and unlocked the manacles on his wrists. His body fell to the ground, still clamped down by the leg irons on his ankles. Stretching him out, they locked his hands into a pair of cuffs that had been bolted to the floor. He was spread-eagled. Ginny wondered if they'd measured him beforehand because the cuffs at both hands and feet held him perfectly still.

The youngest of the trio, Robbie, looked closely at the body stretched out at their feet. "He's not dead, is he?"

"Nah! He's not dead. Just dazed."

"Shut up and gimme that hose!"

Robbie bent down and handed the hose to Drew. He turned the nozzle on, and taking care not to hit the glass behind which the witnesses sat, he aimed the hose at Andy's face. The water went up his nostrils and he choked on it, coming to for the moment. His head thrashed back and forth as he groaned.

Drew turned off the hose and squatted down next to his grandmother's murderer. Lifting Andy's head off the floor, he looked him in the eye. "You killed my grandmother!"

"It's too late . . . " Andy moaned.

"She was so old and helpless . . . "

"Got a date with fate . . . "

Drew stood up abruptly, dropping Andy's head so that it hit the concrete floor with a thump that resounded through the viewing room. Gary went over to the door and picked up the second wooden box. Opening this, he took out a round metal bucket with a flat cover and handed it to Drew. A faint noise came from the bucket that Ginny could not place.

Drew held the pail and spoke to the broken man lying on the floor, his body red and swollen from hundreds of bee stings, his breath coming in gasps as he tried to survive the insect toxins.

"We're not murderers," the young man said. "Not like you. But we brought your death along with us . . . in this bucket? Wanna see?"

Silently, he slid the cover off to the side just a bit, and Ginny suddenly understood the faint noise she'd been hearing as a paw snaked out, its sharp claws extended. She closed her eyes for a moment, then opened them again. It was her duty to watch this to the end.

Inside the concrete room, Drew turned the bucket over and placed it on Andy's abdomen. Then he slid the cover off, leaving the bucket open on top of his victim. The rat inside scratched at the walls, trying to find its way out. Andy grimaced, a trickle of blood ran out from under the rim of the bucket.

"It's really hungry," Drew said.

"Ravenous," said Gary.

Andy screamed.

◆ ◆ ◆

The courtroom was silent. Wallace sat at the defendant's table with Marilyn Hunter next to him. Silently, he prayed that she was a good lawyer. Marsha was on the stand; he wished he could have spared her. When, under questioning by his lawyer, she'd insisted that their relationship was purely professional, he'd understood. He knew that Marilyn had tried to make her admit to more, but she was protecting her marriage. He hoped she could stand up to the D.A.'s questioning. The prosecutor—not James Farrell, he noted—was on her feet.

"So Mrs. Drummond, you claim that you were with Mr. Wallace in his office on September 6th between 2:30 and 3:30 PM. Is that correct?"

"Yes," Marsha said, "he was with me."

"In his office?" Ginny Ormond inquired.

"Yes."

"Really? And what were you two doing?"

Marsha turned her brown eyes in his direction and Wallace looked down. "Talking. Dr. Wallace is a psychologist."

The prosecutor moved closer to the witness. "So you were seeing him in a professional capacity, is that so?"

"Well . . . yes."

"And how long did you say you had been seeing him?"

"Several months."

Ginny turned back to the prosecution's table and picked up a large book that Wallace recognized as his appointment book. He looked at Marilyn. Her face was impassive.

"Do you recognize this book, Mrs. Drummond?" She didn't wait for an answer. "This is Wallace's appointment book. Do you see your name listed on September 6th?"

Marsha's voice was small. "No."

"Well, if you had an appointment to see your psychologist, wouldn't your name be in his appointment book?"

The pretty young woman on the stand just shrugged.

"What was that, Mrs. Drummond? Answer the question please: If you had an appointment to see your psychologist, wouldn't your name be in his appointment book?"

"I suppose so."

"Do you think that perhaps his staff didn't write it down?

"Perhaps."

The prosecutor thumbed through the book and then handed the book to Marsha. "I don't see your name in here anywhere. Can you point out a single appointment that was written in this book?"

Marsha held the book in her hands and abruptly burst into tears.

"Isn't it true that you weren't really there at all, Mrs. Drummond? Aren't you just trying to cover for Wallace because you're having an affair with him? Did you and he plan to get rid of his son together? Was his wife next?"

Marilyn jumped to her feet. "Your Honor, I object. The prosecutor is browbeating the witness!"

The Judge frowned. "Sustained. Continue, Ms. Ormond, without making unfounded remarks."

Oh she was smooth, that prosecutor, Wallace thought. She just smiled and went on. "Yes, your Honor. I'm sorry." Turning back to the witness, she continued. "Mrs. Drummond. Were you having an affair with Wallace?

Marsha was completely intimidated; Wallace could see that on her face. "Yes," she admitted.

"And did you often come to his office in the afternoons?"

"No."

"Where did you go together?"

"We went to motels . . . "

Ginny smiled. "So you weren't in the office during the time in question, were you?"

"No," Marsha admitted.

"You lied about that, didn't you? In fact, we don't know how we can trust you about anything. You've already lied at least once under oath. What other lies have you told us?"

Marsha shook her head. "I didn't . . . I . . . "

"No more questions, your Honor."

"Ms. Hunter, do you wish to redirect?" the judge asked.

As Marilyn got to her feet, Wallace closed his eyes. How had this gone so badly?

"Mrs. Drummond . . . Marsha . . . I know this is hard for you. I understand that you wanted to protect your husband and family. But Dr. Wallace's life may be at stake, and that must take precedence. Were you in a motel room with Dr. Wallace between 2:30 and 3:30 PM on September 6th?"

"Yes," Marsha answered, glaring at Ginny Ormond.

"What was the name of the motel?"

"The Colony."

"Did you register under your own names?"

"No. Of course not."

"Thank you, Mrs. Drummond."

Wallace did not look at Marsha Drummond as she left the witness stand. His eyes were on Lindsey who looked directly at his mistress, her stance radiating the anger and betrayal she felt. Behind Lindsey sat Mike Braun, who leaned forward, his vicious smile showing his enjoyment of the proceedings.

◆ ◆ ◆

James Farrell's red Corvette would stand out in any neighborhood, but in this one it looked particularly out of place. He parked in front of Amy Copeland's house and looked up and down the street. Not much you could tell from here, he thought, and he got out of the car.

Walking around the house, he went into the backyard and looked over the shrubs to see the houses on either side. Two nondescript buildings, their windows reflective, revealing nothing.

Turning, he climbed the back stairs and knocked on the door. There was no answer. He guessed he'd try to talk to Amy's mother later. In the meantime, he wanted to talk to the neighbor mentioned in the police report.

Going around the house to the front, he crossed the driveway and walked up to the front porch of the house next door. At his knock, Bill Stokes, wearing jeans and a plaid shirt, opened the door.

"Sorry to disturb you Mr . . . Stokes. I'm investigating the disappearance of Amy Copeland. You . . . "

"I already spoke to the police," the man answered gruffly.

"I know. I just had a few more questions I wanted to ask you. You mind?"

"No. Come on in. I don't have long though. I have to be at work at four."

Farrell wiped his feet on the mat and entered the small living room. It was neat and nondescript. Some kind of jazz played softly in the background. "So, you work nights?"

"Yeah," Stokes answered, as he lit a cigarette. "The four to midnight shift. I'm with the water district."

"And did you go to work on the day that Amy turned up missing?"

"I already told the police it was my day off."

Farrell shook his head. "Oh sorry. There's so much paperwork. It's hard to keep it all straight. So it was your day off. Were you home all afternoon?"

"No. I went shopping around 3 or 4."

"Now I remember. You showed the police a receipt from the store where you shop. It had the date and time on it."

"That's right," Stokes replied.

Farrell sighed. "So you didn't see anything suspicious?"

Stokes stared at him and shook his head slowly and deliberately.

"Did you know Amy well?"

"Nah. Fixed her bike once is all."

Farrell didn't like him; didn't trust him; and had absolutely nothing on him. "Well thanks, Mr. Stokes. If you think of anything I should know, give me a call, all right?" He handed over a card and let himself out. For the most part, he felt a bit foolish. The police had already done this and they were better trained at it than he. What did he think he was going to accomplish anyway?

◆ ◆ ◆

Down in the basement, Amy gave up struggling for the moment. She was dirty and dusty with tracks of tears running through the grime on her face. She'd heard the door open and close twice. She'd heard the footsteps above her. She'd tried to wriggle free of her bonds and to scream through the duct tape, but no one could hear her.

CHAPTER TWELVE

The wooded area where Ricky Wallace had been murdered was no longer roped off, but there were remnants of crime scene tape on the ground. Farrell studied the printouts of photographs from the scene and tried to orient himself. He looked at a patch of ground and tried to envision the scene that had ended in the boy's death.

Sighing, he shuffled through the papers one more time before deciding to pack it in. What did he think he'd find anyway? The police had been over it like a swarm of locusts.

◆ ◆ ◆

But later, as Farrell ate his hamburger and fries, and went over the police files for the twenty-third time, he decided that whether there was much likelihood or not of his finding anything new, it was important for him to study each of the crime scenes. The first had been small and had yielded nothing, but the second was so large, it seemed possible that the police might have missed something, so he went over it slowly.

The abandoned warehouse was full of rubbish and he'd looked over every broken piece of wood, plaster, and yellow-painted pipe in the room where the murder had taken place with an eye toward minute detail. The chair surrounded by machine parts. What was that all about? The outline on the floor where the body had been found was still there, complete with blood stains. Farrell was used to gory sights; as D.A. he'd visited many a crime scene, but the size of the outline and the pictures of Jimmy Braddock's body were making him queasy. Or maybe it was the hamburger. Or the dust in the room.

There were sneaker footsteps in the dust that the police had preserved. They led to a broken window through which the killer had apparently escaped the building. It was about five feet off the ground, so he went out the door and walked around to the back of the building. At the corner, he stopped to study the broken window and the small yard. By the time the teenagers had entered the building, the murderer was gone. The police had, of course, searched the yard and the surrounding lots, but nothing had been found inside or out except the footprints. And that single hair.

The concrete block wall had once been topped with barbed wire, but most of that was gone. It looked too high to climb, but with adrenaline as a boost? Maybe. If he were the killer, he'd be running, and he'd look for the quickest and easiest way to disappear. On one side of the yard was the street and a chain link fence; on the other another chain link fence. While these were easier to climb, either choice would leave the killer highly visible. Backing up, Farrell started at the window and ran straight for the wall, using his forward momentum to jump, get a foot in a crevice, and grab the top. He fell back down, landing on both feet, but he felt sure that the killer could have made it over. After all, he'd had a lot more reason to make it. There was nowhere else to go.

On the side of the building, Farrell found a couple concrete blocks, and he carried these over to the wall to give himself a step up. The idea was to get a look at the terrain from high up. But there was no way. Just the thought of standing on top of that wall made his mouth go dry and his hands start shaking. Sighing, he abandoned the plan and went around the front, cursing this weakness every hot, dusty step of the way. Ever since he was a kid, he'd been afraid of heights, embarrassed in front of girls in the movies, afraid to walk out on a balcony. Frowning, he pushed the thoughts away and forced himself back to the present.

The abandoned warehouse was surrounded by fences, chain link at the front and two sides, and the concrete one on which he'd been planning to stand, at the back. Walking around the outside of the fenced property, he approached the back wall from the other side. There was a small office building behind the wall, and next to that was a retail shop. He looked at the windowless back of the office building and started walking along that side of the wall.

It was a little used area, with scrubby grass and bushes growing against the concrete blocks. If he were the killer, he'd stay as far from the street as possible, and the bushes, though not offering much in the way of cover, were better than nothing. The wall came to an end a few hundred yards from the warehouse. He'd passed through the yards of several retail shops and a small strip center. On the next street were houses. From here on the killer would be fully exposed. Looking down, Farrell walked back the way he'd come and then turned to follow the wall to its end once again. This time he studied the ground next to the wall, the leaves, bits of trash, and grass underfoot. Nothing . . . nothing . . . nothing . . . . Something? A flash of institutional yellow. Farrell backed up and approached it again. There it was. Carefully, he squatted and moved some leaves and wind-blown trash aside. Under the crumpled, rain-washed remains of a Marlboro carton, was a long piece of lead pipe painted the same yellow as those that littered the floor of the warehouse. And along the jagged edge of the pipe was a dark, brownish-reddish stain.

Farrell backed up. Taking out his cell phone, he dialed police headquarters and asked for Detective Bob Chessman. "This is James Farrell, Detective. I'm out here at the site of the Braddock killing, and I think I've . . . I may have found something. Come out here, will you?"

◆ ◆ ◆

Amy's eyes opened wide as the door at the top of the stairs opened and Stokes came down. Taking a seat on the bottom step, he smiled at her. "I bet you'd like to go home," he said.

The little girl lifted her head and looked at him. Her eyes filled with tears.

"Would you like to go home?"

The child could only nod vehemently.

"I could let you go, couldn't I? You'd never tell on me, would you?"

Amy shook her head.

"No, you wouldn't tell on me, because if you did, I might hurt your mother like I hurt your cat . . . . Come on, scoot over. I'll untie you.

Amy froze. He knew she couldn't move. Stokes got up and drew closer. Squatting down, he untied her legs from the pole and then began to untie her hands. She could feel the bonds loosening, and was tensed to jump up and run, when she felt them tighten up again. "Nah. On the other hand, maybe you're not that smart."

Amy nodded her head, pleading with her eyes. She was that smart. Then she shook her head. No, she would never tell.

"Nah. You're just a dumb kid. You'd go home crying and tell everything."

Desperate, because she knew he wasn't going to let her go, she scrambled to her feet and stumbled up the stairs. The pain in her legs was excruciating. At the top, she banged on the locked door, collapsing against it when she realized it wouldn't open. Would never open in what was left of her short life. Stokes' big hands picked her up and carried her back down. She struggled and kicked, but he laid his big leg across hers and tied her kicking limbs together again.

"Come on, Suse," he laughed. "It's just a game. I like games. Don't you?"

October 17th, 2:28 PM

Ginny Ormond was slowly tightening the noose around John Wallace's neck, and she was enjoying the process enormously.

"Dr. Hewett," she said. "You said the footprints found at the scenes of Ricky Wallace's and Jimmy Braddock's murders match each other. Is that correct?"

"Yes, it is," the witness answered. "Both footprints were made by the same sneakers.

"And do these two footprints also match the sneakers found in Wallace's car?"

"Yes, they do."

"Thank you, Dr. Hewett," Ginny smiled. Although she knew it was weak, she hadn't revealed that weakness to the jury.

"Your witness, Ms. Hunter," said the judge, and Marilyn stood up and approached the stand. Ginny wondered if she would be able to repair the damage she'd just done.

"Dr. Hewett, I only have one question. Could the prints have been made by a different Nike of the same model?"

"Well, Dr. Wallace's sneakers were almost new, and the prints were from a fairly new sneaker. With almost no wear marks, it's difficult . . . so . . . yes, it's possible . . . There is a margin of error in this as in everything."

"So there's no real proof that my client made these prints with *his* Nike sneakers, is there?"

"There is some doubt," Hewett replied.

"Thank you, Doctor. I have no more questions for this witness, Your Honor."

◆ ◆ ◆

It had been a hard day and Marilyn was tired. She thought she'd go straight home and try to forget the whole thing for a few hours. Dinner, some brain-numbing pap on TV and then . . . bed. As she opened the courthouse door, several microphones were pointed at her face.

"Ms. Hunter, don't you think murderers of children should be. . ."

Marilyn turned on the reporter. "The trial is not over and Dr. Wallace is still innocent until proven guilty!"

Another reporter pushed forward in that grappling mob. "But isn't it true that blood stains found at the scene of the last murder match Wallace's?"

That was infuriating. "No! It's not tr . . . "

But they didn't really want her to speak. Still another reporter yelled, "Isn't it true that Wallace has a history of pedophilia?"

Marilyn stopped dead and drew a bead on that last reporter, her eyes flaming. "These are very irresponsible allegations. There is no such history, no such evidence and no proof that Dr. Wallace is guilty of this crime."

The press didn't care. They continued to harass her with ridiculous incendiary questions until she got into her car and slammed the door.

♦ ♦ ♦

The fluorescent lights flickered over the drab colors, metal sur-
faces, and sharp edges of the police lab. It was all so cold, it
made Farrell more conscious of the heated passions of the oc-
cupants. The pipe he'd found by the wall had been gently
picked up and transported by Detective Chessman, so that their
forensic experts could examine it thoroughly.

"It's type A," Hewitt said.

"You sure?" Chessman should have known better.

"No," Hewett said. "I was just joking. Of course, I'm sure.
I've only been doing this for twenty years."

"Wallace is type O," Farrell stated. Of course, they all knew
that. Too bad red cells had no DNA.

Chessman scratched his neck. "We don't really have any
proof that this pipe was involved in the killing."

"It's the same type of piping that's all over that warehouse . . . and the same paint," Farrell reminded him.

"And the blood is about three weeks old," said Hewett.

"Yeah. But there aren't any useful prints," Chessman said.
"We already think the killer was wearing gloves, but it
would've really helped if we'd been able to get even one print
belonging to the boy."

Farrell sighed.

♦ ♦ ♦

Even though he was on leave of absence, it was still a bit shocking to see Ginny sitting at his desk. She had her feet up and was
reading a brief.

"Don't get too comfortable," he said.

Ginny smiled. She was so beautiful, Farrell couldn't help
being glad to see her again, couldn't help wanting to kiss those
luscious lips. Despite his misgivings.

He walked in and shut the door behind him. Turning to face her he was gratified to see that at least she'd taken her feet off the desk. "I've found some new evidence," he said. "Wallace may be in the clear."

Ginny shook her head and chuckled. "Oh really? When did you take up police work, Farrell?"

She was so tough. How was he going to connect with her? "That's not the point. The point is that as long as we assume that Wallace is guilty, we're not looking for the real killer. And that killer may be holding the little Copeland girl. We have no body. She might be alive!"

Ginny stretched in the chair like a cat, her white silk blouse clinging to her curves. "Farrell, come on. Amy Copeland does not fit . . . "

" . . . the profile. Yes, I know. But I found a pipe with blood on it at the scene of the Braddock murder. It's type A and Wallace is type O. Somewhere there's a type A sonofabitch who was hit with a lead pipe by a boy trying to defend himself. And what if he has Amy? What if the police are looking in all the wrong places because you're not making the connection?"

Ginny stood up and stepped closer to him. "I'm prosecuting this care, Farrell. Not defending it. You can suppose all you want, but until I have someone else to prosecute, Wallace is it. You know that."

Farrell wanted to shake her. He knew how hidebound the department could be. He knew how they'd want to avoid embarrassment at any cost. But would they go so far as to convict an innocent man? "This is your big break," he said. "Isn't it? In my place, you can finally go for the jugular. Even if it's the wrong man. Doesn't really matter, does it? As long as it's a man."

Ginny was way too sophisticated for that one to break through. She just smiled suggestively and drew closer.

"Come on, James," she said softly. "I like men. Why don't you take me out to dinner, and I'll remind you how much I like men."

Her arms went around his neck and he could feel her warmth against the length of his body. He could also feel himself starting to respond, so he lifted her arms from his neck and backed up. Ginny started to move forward, but he held up a warning hand. "There's a man in jail for something he didn't do, and a little girl who's dead or in deadly danger." His voice was soft, but his body language was not.

Ginny lifted a delicate shoulder and tilted her head toward it, her shrug both elegant and eloquent. She walked around to the other side of the desk and took her place in his chair. Her face was a mask when she finally spoke. "Is there anything else, Mr. Farrell?"

◆ ◆ ◆

Sean Copeland, despite his air of disdain, which was a defense he'd cultivated since his father had left home, was deeply disturbed by the disappearance of his little sister. He sat on the stoop in his backyard watching the glow of his cigarette. He didn't know what to do, but there had to be something. His mother was falling apart before his eyes. It wasn't his fault this time. Yeah, she was a loser, but she was his mom and he couldn't just sit there and let her have a nervous breakdown, could he? But what was he supposed to do? He didn't know anything. Couldn't find out anything.

He took a drag and the light of the cigarette filled the darkness. But then a light snapped on next door, so bright that he disappeared in it. It was that guy, what was his name? Stock . . . man, Stone, Stokes, that was it. Stokes carried a brown paper bag onto his porch and down the stairs. He held it away from his body as if it were diseased or something. Opening the trash can, he dropped it with a thud, then replaced the lid. Sean crushed his cigarette against the concrete stoop. Didn't want to be seen.

After Stokes went inside and turned off the light, Sean got up and sauntered over to the man's yard. The light was dim, just a sliver of moonlight, but it was enough to see to pull open the bag that his neighbor had just deposited in the trash can. Whew! It stunk. It took him a moment to make out what it was. It was bent all wrong, but when he turned it . . . Oh shit!

Sean jumped back, dropping the lid of the can with a loud clatter. The light on the porch went back on and he melted quickly into the darkness, frozen in place as Stokes came back down the stairs and replaced the lid of the can.

"Damn cats!" the man exclaimed.

After Stokes had gone back inside, Sean started to breathe again. There was no doubt that the two dead eyes staring up at him from inside the trash had belonged to Angel, his sister's cat.

◆ ◆ ◆

Inside the house, he could hear his mother crying softly in her room. He wondered if she'd cry like that if he were missing, but then it just really didn't matter. No one should feel like she was feeling.

The hall phone was close to her room, so he had to whisper. "Vinny! Hey Vinny, it's Sean."

"Hey man! Where you been? You was supposed to . . . "

"Yeah! I know. Listen, fuck that. You know that gun you got? I want to borrow it."

"Borrow it?" Vinny laughed. "What the hell for?"

"Because I want to borrow it. You don't need to know. Okay? Just bring it over to my house."

"Hell no. You think I got nothing better to do than run errands for you?"

Sean wanted to grab him through the phone and choke him. "Come on, Vinny. You know I got no car. Bring it now. It's important."

◆ ◆ ◆

He waited impatiently out front for Vinny to drive up. It seemed like it was taking forever. He'd already gone through six cigarettes. A screech of tires coming around the block let him know the wait was over, and then Vinny's shiny black Chevy skidded to a stop in front of his house. Sean was already at the curb as Vinny opened the window.

"What took you so long?"

Vinny grinned, letting Sean peek at the gun in his lap. "So you gonna tell me what it's for?"

Sean shook his head.

"Come on! I want in!"

"It's not money," Sean said. "Just give it to me. I'll give it back tomorrow . . . Come on, dude. I gotta go."

Although he looked doubtful, Vinny handed the gun over, then rolled up the window and stepped on the gas.

Sean held the gun against his body and casually walked back toward his front stoop, sitting down and bringing the gun to his lap. It was dark on the stoop, and he could barely see it. He was going to open the door and go inside, when the garage door of Stokes' house opened, and Stokes came out and getting into his car, drove it into the garage.

Sean reacted instantly, getting up and moving through the shadows to stand just outside the open garage door and peek inside. Stokes had gotten out of the car and had opened the trunk. Sean slipped the gun into the waistband of his jeans in back. He listened for the footsteps leaving, and then the garage door began to close. Taking a deep breath, he rolled under the door and crouched at the back of the car. The door to the house was closed. Should he follow Stokes inside, or wait here?

◆ ◆ ◆

Stokes moved deliberately. He strode down the stairs to the basement, and turned on the light. It was okay because the windows had been taped over so no light could escape and no one could peek in. The little girl was laying on the floor in a puddle of urine. Stokes wrinkled his nose. She stunk. He thought getting rid of the dead cat would improve the smell in here, but it hadn't. Shit, he had half a mind to dump her in the trash with her stinky cat. But no, he had other plans for this one.

He liked the way she looked asleep. Except for all the dirt on her face. Picking her up, he slung her over his shoulder and carried her up the stairs and through the house to the garage. She was awake by the time he laid her in the trunk, her eyes wide. This was going to be fun. He slammed the trunk lid closed and got in the car. Then opened the garage and backed out. Yep, this was going to really be fun.

◆ ◆ ◆

Sean lay on the floor in the back of the car trying not to breathe. He thought it might be best to just blow a hole in the guy from behind, but then the car was moving fast before he could get the gun into his hand. And then because he'd been buried under a blanket on the floor, he hadn't actually seen what Stokes put in the trunk. What if it wasn't Amy? What if he killed the man in cold blood and all he'd done was kill a cat? So he waited to see what would happen.

The car began to shudder and jerk, so Sean realized they were driving off the road. He tried not to gasp as he was slammed into the hump on the floor of the car repeatedly. He was sure he was bruised and that his stomach would no longer be able to digest food when the car finally lurched to a stop. The driver's door opened and Stokes got out, his feet stepping on what sounded like gravel. Something, probably a branch, slapped the side of the car. Then the trunk opened and he could feel the suspension rise as something heavy was lifted out. Footsteps in the gravel again, this time fading into the distance. Sean pulled the blanket off his head and sat up, peering out of the windows. On one side of the car were several bushes screening it from the road. On the other was some kind of wooden structure. He'd have to get out of the car to see more.

♦ ♦ ♦

Stokes put Amy down on the ground and removed the rope that was coiled around his shoulders. He'd taken it out of the trunk before he'd picked up the girl. As he already knew, there was no way up the watertower without that rope. The ladder had been cut off about ten feet up so that kids wouldn't be able to climb it. Taking careful aim, he threw the rope with the grappling hook on the end upward. He'd practiced this often, but the first try was a miss. On the second try, the hook grabbed and he pulled on the rope to make sure it was tight.

Getting Amy up there wasn't going to be hard either. He tied the other end of the rope underneath the girl's arms, and her weight held the rope taut. It wasn't hard for him to climb it and get to that first rung, though from the sounds below him, it probably threw her back and forth a bit as his weight shifted. Tough shit.

When he was solidly settled on the ladder, Stokes released the grappling hook and began pulling up Amy. When he had her neatly-tied-up body safely in his arms, he rolled up the rope and left it there so it would be available when he was ready to go home.

◆ ◆ ◆

Amy could hardly breathe. She wanted to scream, but the tape on her mouth made it impossible. Tears ran down her cheeks into her nostrils, and she thought she'd choke. Her nose was so stuffed from crying, and the tape was so tight. She was dizzy with the swaying and was afraid she'd throw up and die in her own vomit. Could that happen to people? Where was Mommy?

She could hardly understand what she was seeing. The ground kept getting farther and farther away. The man was climbing a ladder. Where was he taking her? Where was Mommy? Why didn't somebody save her? She knew he was going to kill her. He'd killed Angel. Maybe he'd killed her mommy too. No, no, no. She couldn't believe that. Not Mommy. Not Sean.

She tried to be calm. If she could only be calm, maybe her nose would unswell and let more air in. She needed more air.

Suddenly, there was the crack of wood, and Amy felt her body lurch out over the abyss. The ground whirled beneath her, and she looked up to see that the man was holding her by the ropes around her feet. Was he going to drop her? The rope was slipping!

Her body was jolted as the rope around one ankle came undone. She could feel the remaining rope digging into her ankle as it bore her full weight. She could feel it taking the skin off the top of her foot as gravity relentlessly pulled her down. Mommy! She silently screamed. Mommy! Mommy!

◆ ◆ ◆

John Wallace lay on his bunk behind the bars of his cell and listened to a famous talk show host interviewing his wife. He knew that the prison guard thought he was a man who had murdered his own child, so he wasn't surprised when the sound was turned up so he could better hear what they were saying.

"Mrs. Wallace, I know this is difficult for you, so take your time. Your son is dead and your husband is on trial for his murder. He's admitted to having an affair. How do you feel?"

How do you think she feels, you shit, Wallace thought.

"I feel . . . betrayed . . . and . . . angry. He lied to me. I don't even know who he is anymore."

"Before this all happened, Wallace seemed to be an upstanding citizen. He counseled prisoners. He protested violence and the loss of human rights. In fact, we have a clip of an interview."

Wallace groaned and pulled his pillow over his head, but he could still hear his own voice.

"We are a violent society, and we seem to believe that we can change this by harnessing violence and using it against itself. But what's the difference between violence imposed by society and violence perpetrated against society? It's still violence. We cannot answer brutality and cruelty in kind. As all our greatest leaders, from Jesus to Buddha to Mahatma Ghandi and Martin Luther King, have told us, the only answer to violence is to turn the other cheek."

The talk show host on the clip had been amused.

"So we should let murderers go free?"

"Of course not. Murderers should be imprisoned and kept away from the society of others. I'm saying that we should not answer violence with violence. Instead we should go to the root, to the cause—the violence and inequities of our social system—and begin to change it where it can be changed. Through education. Through social reform Through the genuine care of one individual for another . . . "

"So Mrs. Wallace," the host continued. "Is this the man you married?"

Lindsey's voice had tears in it. "I thought it was."

Wallace could hardly contain the rage in his heart at the injustice that was being done to him and to her as the talk show went on. Why would she agree to do it? Was she that unforgiving? Did she hate him that much?

"The man we saw in that clip was against the Eye-for-an-Eye law. He founded the organization, S.E.E., to try and stop its passage. What do you think he feels about it now?"

Mercifully, the guard must have lost interest because the sound stopped. Wallace turned to the wall and tried to disappear.

◆ ◆ ◆

Stokes's hands were on Amy's ankle and on her leg, and he was pulling her up. He'd saved her! He threw her over his shoulder and continued to climb, but even though her legs were now untied she didn't fight him. It would be so easy for him to just drop her.

◆ ◆ ◆

At the top of the ladder, Stokes turned to look down at the two-hundred foot drop. He hadn't planned on that rotten rung. That was close. He'd almost lost her, and then what would have happened? No game. Nothing. The whole thing would have been a waste of time. Fortunately, all those years at the gym had paid off.

Although most of the railing was rotted, the floor was mostly solid. He'd been up here many times before, so he knew exactly where, and where not, to step.

◆ ◆ ◆

On the ground, Sean was desperately searching for a way to climb the ladder. There were no trees close enough, no logs he could move. He'd seen the furtive figure with the small body slung over its shoulder, and he'd seen that small body swing out and almost fall. A short piece of rope had fallen instead and with his heart in his teeth, he'd picked it up, but couldn't see a way to use it. Maybe he could tie it to the top of a tree and pull it down so that he could inch out on the trunk and get to the ladder, but there weren't any trees close enough.

It occurred to him to go for help, but he didn't know where he was. Maybe he could take Stokes' car. But then by the time he could convince someone to help him, it would be all over and his little sister would be dead. Maybe he could back the car under the ladder!

Sean ran back to the car and opened the driver door. There were no keys in the ignition. Frantically, he searched under the seat, almost in tears with frustration. No keys. No keys. But then his hand hit a lever and the trunk popped open. Okay. Maybe there was something in the trunk.

Getting off his knees, he ran to the back of the car and saw it immediately. A rope with a grappling hook on the end. Stokes came prepared. Sean grabbed the rope by the hook and raced back to the ladder. Wildly he threw the hook at the rung five feet over his head.

◆ ◆ ◆

Two hundred feet above him, Stokes set Amy down on a wooden slatted floor laid across the inside supports of the tank and quickly struck a match that he used to light a small lantern hanging from one of the struts. Yellow light filled the interior of the tank. Beneath them the smooth inner walls sloped down toward a black gaping emptiness. Stokes looked over at Amy, then crouched down next to her and pulled off the tape.

The little girl's screams reverberated off the curving walls.

Stokes smiled. "Scream all you like. No one can hear you. That's why I like it here."

"Please. Please," Amy begged. "I want to go home. I'm scared . . . I'm hungry . . . "

"Yeah, and you smell too. But go ahead. Beg me. Isn't this a good game? My brothers used to say that when they tied me up and left me in the closet. Isn't this a good game?"

"It's not a good game!" Amy screamed. "It's a mean game! You're mean!"

Stokes laughed and sat down on the slats. "You look funny when you screw up your face like that! You know, Susan, you're the mean one. I like to make you beg."

The little girl looked at him queerly. "I'm not Susan," she said.

Oh sure. Like he was going to believe that. She never could be trusted. He got up and moved toward her. "Of course you are, Susan. Susan the bitch! Susan, you shouldn't have let them do that! I thought you loved me . . . "

"I'm not Susan," Amy cried. "I'm Amy! Amy!"

Stokes' eyes narrowed. He knew her game. "Well, Jeffy's not here to protect you anymore. So, you'd better be good and play the way I say."

Amy retreated against the wall of the tank. She almost could disappear if she made herself small enough. But she'd never be able to get away from him.

◆ ◆ ◆

Down below, Sean had finally hooked the lowest rung of the ladder and was now attempting to climb the wildly swinging rope. On his first, second, and third attempts he fell. Then stood gasping for breath. He could do it. He knew he could do it.

◆ ◆ ◆

Outside the jail, two groups faced each other. In one group were members of S.E.E., Jack Decker among them. Jack had known and admired Wallace for years. If not for the Doc, he'd have probably landed in jail himself . . . or worse. Probably be an addict and a bum. When Wallace had asked him to join S.E.E., he'd been proud to do so. Now, with Wallace in jail and the law a fact, Decker was more determined than ever to fight it. Now he was working not only for what was right, but for his friend. He owed him.

The two groups of people were screaming at each other, no one listening to anyone. Jack couldn't stand the signs the supporters of the law were holding: "Kill murderers!" "Make them pay!" "Kill them before they kill you!" And now they'd added a new one to their repertoire: "Kill Wallace!" It burned Jack up just to see it.

"You don't really think they'll get their hands on Wallace, do you?" he shouted into the noise and turmoil.

"He'll win!" the guy next to him added.

Three feet away, someone holding a "Kill Wallace!" sign yelled, "Fuck you!"

Another guy, a big muscular type he'd seen before, pushed his way forward and into Jack's way, "He's guilty! He's gonna die!"

"Not in a million years!" Decker yelled back.

The big guy just stabbed his sign upward. "Wallace is dead! Wallace is dead!"

"Yeah Braun!" A supporter screamed approval. "Wallace is dead!"

Another voice chimed in and then the whole group was chanting. What could Jack do but begin his own chant? "Wallace will win! Wallace will win!" He felt his heart swell as the other protesters took up the cry and added their voices to his.

Louder and louder they screamed until Jack felt he was swimming in a lake of noise.

"Shut up you motherfuckers!" the man called Braun boomed.

"Wallace will win!"

"Shut up, I said!"

Jack and his group continued to yell, and Braun bent over, picked up a rock and hurled it at them.

CHAPTER THIRTEEN

The lights snapped on and Farrell and Marilyn stepped into his kitchen. While he made space on the oak table for the box of documents and the Chinese food he was carrying, Marilyn opened the most likely drawer.

"That one," he said, pointing with his chin as he set the food down.

Marilyn glanced his way, opened the correct drawer and pulled out two forks. Those little movements—the turn of her head, the swing of her hair, the fact of her making herself at home in his kitchen—all conspired to set his blood roaring in his veins.

In a heartbeat, Farrell closed the small space between them, and as she turned, he caught her in his arms. Her face changed subtly as he pulled her closer, going from open and friendly to soft and mysterious. He leaned in and delicately touched his lips to hers. They were supple and yielding. He grew more insistent. The forks she held clattered to the floor as he peeled off her suit jacket and pushed her against the counter. He could feel her all along the entire length of his body. And he wanted her with every cell, every muscle, every organ and gland. Her response had been immediate and seemed every bit as powerful. That knowledge alone drove him forward.

His lips kissed her mouth, her neck, her temples, her mouth again. His tongue tasted her and he was willing and ready to be consumed.

She leaned her head back, revealing the soft vulnerability of her throat. He kissed her there as well.

"James," she whispered. "Oh James." Her lips against his cheek were warm and moist.

"James," she repeated. "We don't have time for this."

"Oh no," he murmured. "There's always time for this."

He could feel her lips curve into a smile. And he kissed her more ardently than before.

Then she was pulling away. "We don't have time."

Groaning, he let her go, willing the needful ache to subside. The growing distance between their bodies helped, and in a few minutes, they both had themselves under control. "Okay," he said. "You're right."

She laughed. "Want a raincheck?"

"In writing," Farrell grinned.

Laughing, they opened up the food containers, got fresh forks from the drawer and sat down to do what they'd come to do. Between bites, Marilyn read aloud through the police reports piled on the table.

"Wait a minute," Farrell said. "Read me that bit again."

"Which bit?"

"Hard evidence."

"Hard evidence. Okay: footprints, a few threads . . . and of course, the hair."

"Forget the hair. I don't for one second believe that Wallace was at the scene of that murder."

Marilyn grimaced. "Yeah. But where'd the hair come from then?"

Shaking his head, Farrell picked up another forkful of lo mein. "I don't know. I just don't know. Whenever I think about it I see Ginny Ormond taking that package from Glen Morgan. But I just don't see a connection."

"Okay. So skip the hair."

"Yeah. We've got footprints, a few threads . . . it's not much to go on. I'm missing something. I feel like I should be putting two and two together somehow, but I'm not doing it. Footprints . . . a few threads. What color?

Marilyn went through the papers again and found the report on the threads. "Here it is. It says they have five threads: two gold, two pink and one navy blue. They're 100% cotton.

Farrell studied the ceiling, willing his brain to make sense of it all. "Two gold, one blue . . . and a cut made by a jagged pipe . . . "

Then he saw it, just a flash. A flash of plaid.

"What is it?" Marilyn asked.

"I've seen a shirt with those colors . . . "

Suddenly Farrell dropped his fork on the table and was on his feet and running for the door. "Stokes!" he cried. "Amy's next door neighbor! He was wearing a shirt with those colors two days ago when I went to his house. And Marilyn! He had a recently healed cut on his cheek!" He stopped long enough to look at Marilyn still seated at the table. "Come on!"

◆ ◆ ◆

Farrell's car jerked to a stop outside Stokes' house and he and Marilyn jumped out. The house was dark.

Wasting no time, Farrell climbed the stairs to the front porch and banged on the door.

"He's not here," Marilyn said.

Farrell slammed his hand against the door once more, then turned and leaned against the house. "We have to get inside."

"We need a warrant."

He grimaced. "I know that. But if he's not here then he either has Amy with him or he's left her here. Either way, we have to move fast." Farrell looked at her, at them: two lawyers who knew the law very well, who upheld the law every day of their lives. Marilyn nodded, and turned to see if the front windows would open.

Farrell, seeing that she was in agreement with him, ran back to the car and opened the trunk. She was already heading for the back of the house when he joined her, flashlight and crowbar in hand. At the back of the house, Farrell broke the lock and they entered the kitchen.

"Oh, I can just see the headlines: "DA arrested for breaking and entering . . . ." Marilyn said.

"With accomplice," the DA added.

Marilyn groaned as Farrell flashed the light around the kitchen. Quietly, they checked the lower cabinets and the pantry, then moved on to the rest of the house.

In Stokes' bedroom, there was nothing, but in the laundry basket in the bathroom, they found the plaid shirt with the small tear in the sleeve.

"Oh my God," Marilyn murmured. Farrell stuffed the shirt back into the basket, knowing that the police would have to find it there themselves for it to be of any use as evidence.

At the end of the hall, a door led to the basement and as Farrell shone the light down the stairs, he dreaded what he might find at the bottom. Slowly, with Marilyn at his back, he stepped down into the gloom.

The flashlight revealed a basement, a furnace, a pile of old belongings, and then an empty corner. Farrell moved closer.

"Amy?" Marilyn called softly.

A flash of red told the story and as the two closed in, they could see that Amy had been held in the corner. There was the red hair ribbon, ropes, a roll of duct tape, the smell of urine and feces . . . and maybe something worse.

"Shit!" Farrell yelled, no longer caring about keeping quiet. "Shit! He's taken her somewhere."

"Oh God. Where?"

"I don't know. Somewhere he can do what he wants and not worry about noise . . . . Or somewhere to dispose of the body."

Marilyn's face paled. "I don't see any blood."

Farrell was already halfway up the stairs. In Stokes' bedroom, there had been a desk and he wanted to see what papers he might find there.

Quickly, knowing how urgent everything had suddenly become, they went through the drawers of the desk.

"Look, here's a hospital bill . . . and records." Marilyn said.

"He said he worked for the water district."

"Must be lots of lonely places he could go: pumping stations . . . reservoirs . . . "

Farrell felt the blood drain from his face. "The old water tower."

♦ ♦ ♦

Back in the Corvette, they hastily made plans. Farrell didn't see how he could avoid being the one to go to the water tower to face Stokes while Marilyn would get in touch with the Chief, who for whatever reason, was not answering his cell phone. At Trevino's house, Marilyn jumped out and headed for the front door. The tail lights of the car turned the corner and disappeared.

No one answered her first urgent knock, so Marilyn peered through the glass pane next to the door and looked into the small foyer. She could see pictures of Trevino as a young soldier with his buddies. There were also some framed medals, even a purple heart. Trevino himself, pulling on a robe, walked in front of the display and opened the door. He took a long look at the slightly disheveled woman standing on his porch introducing herself.

"This had better be good, Ms. Hunter. I left work hours ago."

Marilyn pushed past him and into the foyer. Turning, she confronted him with the new evidence. "Farrell and I found the kidnapper of Amy Copeland, and he's also the killer of those boys . . . . Wallace saw a shirt on Bill Stokes, Amy's next door neighbor that matches the threads found at the scene of the Ricky Wallace murder."

Trevino lit a cigarette and inhaled. "Hardly conclusive evidence."

Marilyn pulled a sheet of paper from her pocket. "Captain, there's more: Stokes' hospital records show that he's type A. And he has a recently healed cut on his cheek! All you have to do is get inside the house! I'm sure you'll find more than enough to arrest and convict him."

"Look. I don't know why you and Farrell are out there playing detective, but we have DNA evidence on Wallace. What you're suggesting is all circumstantial. A pipe found near the scene three weeks after the crime. It just doesn't cut it. Now, if you'll excuse me."

Marilyn couldn't believe it. Was he just going to dismiss them? He took her elbow and opened the door, practically shoving her through. "But Captain," she protested.

"Good night, Ms. Hunter."

Marilyn gaped as the door closed, unable to comprehend what had just happened. She was a lawyer; she knew evidence when she saw it. What the hell was going on? Okay, she thought, as she stepped off the walkway and onto the lawn, let's see if we can find out.

Stealthily, she moved across the front of the house and around toward the back. A lighted window drew her attention and she headed for it. She saw that there was a small gap where the blinds did not quite reach the bottom of the window sill. Crouching down, she rested beneath the window, then took a deep breath and slowly rose until her eyes were level with the opening.

They widened as they took in the sight. Trevino was sitting on the bed, his back toward the window, and there was a long-legged woman stretched out beside him, also facing away from the window. "Farrell is not going to let this go," the captain said.

"He'll let it go," the woman replied. "He can't win."

Trevino turned to look at her. "He's got his teeth in it. I'm telling you I have a bad feeling about this."

The woman's hand came up and cupped Trevino's neck pulling him down to her and rolling onto her back. Marilyn gasped as she saw the curve of cheek resolve into Ginny Ormond's face. Trevino, his legs still on the floor, gazed at the woman on his bed, his arms on either side of her, his face full of longing.

Ginny held his head in her hands, and raised herself up to kiss him gently, pushing his robe off his shoulders and revealing his sagging chest and bulging belly. "No one will ever know what you did," she said, "as long as you don't tell them."

Trevino kissed her passionately and she lay back on the pillows, her breasts bared invitingly. "It's all yours, lover. Do whatever you want with it."

Trevino removed the robe, and clumsily pulled his legs up onto the bed, so that he was lying along the length of Ginny's body. He kissed her deeply, worshipping her with his lips.

Marilyn wanted to look away, and when she saw the prosthesis that was Trevino's left leg, she finally did. Sitting down abruptly, she waited a moment for her heart to stop pounding. Then she got up and got away as quickly as her legs would take her.

◆ ◆ ◆

Inside the house, as Trevino practiced the act that had led him to the betrayal of everything he'd ever believed in, the phone rang. He tried to let it keep ringing, but finally picked the receiver up and yelled into it. "What?"

"Captain!" the desk sergeant yelled. "There's a riot at the jail! We've got an angry mob out there!"

Trevino felt his previously flaming parts go cold and small. "Shit. I'll be right there."

◆ ◆ ◆

The police station was in an uproar when Marilyn hurried in. She pushed past heavily armed policemen and into the detectives' offices. Chessman was checking the clip on his gun. He turned as she came up behind him.

"Detective . . . Chessman? I need your help."

◆ ◆ ◆

At the county jail, Mike Braun was in his element. All around him men were brawling with each other, screaming recriminations and throwing rocks. He'd started it with a single rock, and now it had blown up into a full fledged riot as supporters and protesters of the eye-for-an-eye law sought to settle their dispute in blood. He was pushing for the gates of the jail, his aim to get inside and get Wallace. At last, that damned do-gooder who had fingered him and gotten him fired was going to get what he deserved.

The new law would get him anyway, so the way Braun figured it, why wait? The crowd was here; the time was now.

Suddenly the gate was flung open and six guards stepped out into the fray. One fired a shot into the air, but Braun and his men were only inflamed further. With a yell, they surged toward the guards and the open gate, mowing down the protesters who attempted to get in their way.

"Kill Wallace!" Braun screamed, and his chest swelled with pride as the others took up his cry.

The mob pounded toward the gate, beating anyone standing in the way with anything that came to hand: rocks, sticks, and fists. The guards tried to hold the line, but they were falling back before the crowd. The warden stepped forward, a megaphone in hand. "Go home!" He ordered. "This is a government facili . . . "

The rock that Braun threw connected with the warden's head and he went down. With that, the guards retreated and tried to get back inside. But it was too late; Braun and his mob were on top of them. "Kill Wallace!"

One of the guards fired wildly into the crowd, but even though one of the rioters fell, the rest kept going, Braun in the lead. In the prison yard, the guards had regrouped and were doing their best to stop the onslaught, but the crowd was beyond reason or control, and the guards were outnumbered ten to one.

Braun's fist connected with one of the guards and knocked him off his feet. Grabbing his rifle, Braun held it aloft and yelled "Come on!"

Many of the guards were on the ground either crawling for cover or lying still in a pool of blood. As they streamed across the yard and pushed against the door to the jail proper, Braun spotted his ex-coworker, Brian Geary.

"Mike! Stop this!" the guard yelled, thrusting past the others to get to Braun. "Mike! Are you crazy? What are you doing?" He grabbed Braun's arm and tried to turn him from the jail entrance.

Braun shoved Geary aside and pointed the rifle at him when
he attempted to stop him again. "Get away, Geary. Get away
now. While you still can!"

Geary was no hero. He melted backward straight into the
arms of some of Braun's men, who stripped him of his keys and
weapons. Now, armed with keys, rifles and billy clubs, they
were ready to get Wallace.

"Kill Wallace!" they screamed as they poured into the jail.
"Kill Wallace!"

♦ ♦ ♦

Inside his cell, Wallace could hear his name being shouted as
the rioters moved toward him. Frantically, he looked around for
something to use in his own defense.

♦ ♦ ♦

Farrell's car screeched to a halt at the bottom of the water
tower. Jumping out, he ran for the ladder, not realizing until
he was on top of it that it began ten feet above his head.
Confused, he looked around. Maybe this wasn't the right
place after all. Maybe he was on the wrong track. Looking
up, he pondered the ladder again. A glimmer of light in the
darkness high above his head was the assurance he needed.
Of course, this was the place. Now all he had to do was figure out how to get up there. A wave of dizziness at the
thought almost sent him crashing to his knees. He knew
he'd never be able to do it.

♦ ♦ ♦

At the police station, Marilyn had explained everything in a
rush to Chessman, who took it all in, put it all together and became an instant ally. As they rushed through the hallway toward

the parking lot, Chessman yelled, "The water tower is twenty to thirty minutes from here!"

Marilyn didn't bother to answer. They were out of time. She stopped as police cars screeched out of the parking lot, sirens screaming, and lights flashing. Chessman ran for one of the patrol cars, yanking the door open. He was about to fling his bulk into the driver's seat, but a meaty hand grabbed his upper arm and pulled. "That's my car, detective," the big cop said. The other two officers joining forces with the first were just as big, so Chessman gallantly surrendered the vehicle.

All around them, tires were squealing as patrol cars, dodging left and right, vacated the lot. In a moment, the noise had stopped and no cars were left. Marilyn looked around. "Now what?"

"Where's your car?" Chessman asked.

"At Farrell's. Yours?"

"In the shop."

"So. Should we steal one?"

Chessman smiled. "I have a better idea."

◆ ◆ ◆

Stokes was finished with his cigarette. He stubbed it out on the floorboards of the tank. He was ready. "Now, it's time to play," he said, striding toward her.

Amy was sitting on the floor as far away from him as she could get. She stood up and cringed against the sloping wall of the tank. "I don't want to play."

"Susan. Susan. I told you. I say what and when we play."

"I'm not Sus . . . "

In two steps he closed the distance between them and hit her backhanded across the face. "Don't say that again!"

Amy's nose was bleeding, and her eyes were awash with tears. She knew only one emotion: terror. Cowering, she skittered across the floorboards, trying to get out of his way, to get out of his world.

A big hand grabbed her and pulled her to her feet. "Okay. Now you can run away. Go on! Try to get away!"

Amy froze, so he shoved her against the wall of the tank, banging her head against the wood. "Try to get away, I said!"

As she slid down the wall, ready for whatever evil this man had in store for her, she suddenly believed in God, angels, fairies, pixies, magic and everlasting good, everything she'd forgotten since she'd first seen her dead cat and realized that she'd fallen into a trap.

Sean was inside the tank! And he had a gun! "Sean!" she cried. "Oh Sean!"

Stokes had seen him too. "So Jeffy, you got here after all. I thought you were dead."

"Get away from my sister, you fucking pervert!"

Amy didn't care how many f-words he used, as long as he made the bad man go away. She began to pray.

"Tch tch . . . such nasty language," Stokes said.

Sean's finger was straining on the trigger. Amy could see it. He brought his other hand up to steady the one holding the gun. Still the man didn't move. She could see the sweat on Sean's face.

The sound of the gun was so loud, she screamed. But the man was still standing. He grabbed Amy and pulled her in front of him. She struggled, but he held her fast. And now how could Sean shoot him?

◆ ◆ ◆

On the ground, Farrell heard the shot and the scream. Shaking with fear, fury and frustration, he dug a rope out of the trunk of his car and knotted it around a rock. He threw it at the ladder, but he was way off. It fell, almost hitting him on the head. Picking up the rock, he tried again. This time it went wide. The third time, the rock fell through the bottom rung and he tugged it gently into the angle between the upright and the rung. Would it hold? He would have to try. Taking hold of the rope, he laboriously began to pull himself hand over hand toward the ladder. Lucky he was an athlete because otherwise, he thought, this would be impossibly difficult. Then the rung gave way and he fell to the ground.

◆ ◆ ◆

Wallace backed up against the back wall of his cell, trying to melt into the shadows as the crowd got closer. They screamed his name all the way through the jail until they were standing outside his cell. Then they stopped.

A man pounded his cage with a bundle of keys. "I found him!" Wallace recognized him; it was Mike Braun.

"Let's get him!" A rioter yelled.

"Let's kill him!"

"Oh, we're gonna kill him, all right," Braun assured them.

"He deserves to die!"

"Murderer! Child killer!"

Wallace knew he didn't stand a chance against this mob, especially when he looked into Braun's face and saw nothing but hatred.

Braun fitted a key in the lock on the cell door and swung it open, standing back so the crowd could reach him. Wallace cried out his innocence in vain as the mob carried him off.

◆ ◆ ◆

Marilyn didn't know where they were going. Chessman had said he'd had a better idea, so she was following him. They'd taken an elevator and a stairway and were now exiting onto the roof of the police station. A helicopter stood in a circle painted on the flat surface.

Chessman raced across the roof. Yanking the pilot's door open, he pulled himself in, and Marilyn followed suit on the other side of the machine. She was relieved to see the key in the ignition. "He never takes the keys," Chessman said. "Says no one can fly the damn thing, so why bother?"

"Can you fly it?"

Chessman was manipulating the controls, pushing buttons, checking switches. "Sure," he said.

"Are you a pilot?" Marilyn asked as she cinched her seatbelt.

"I flew one in Vietnam."

"Vietnam! That was a long time ago."

Chessman looked at her in triumph as the engine fired up. "They haven't changed that much!"

Marilyn was not reassured. "So were you a pilot or something?"

Chessman smiled. "Or something I guess."

Her heart was racing. She wished she hadn't asked. Overhead the blade was picking up speed. It was very noisy. Chessman put a pair of headphones on his head and motioned for her to do the same.

"I was being lifted to a drop off point. But the pilot was hit, and I had to fly the chopper."

Marilyn stared at him, took the headphones off, undid her seatbelt and swung her legs out the door. "I think we should just get a cab."

But it was too late. The chopper was already rising off the pavement. It canted crazily and she would have fallen out except that Chessman grabbed her by the back of her shirt and pulled her back inside. He grinned and gave her the thumbs up sign. Without further objection, she put on her seatbelt and held on tight as the machine climbed erratically upward.

♦ ♦ ♦

The Corvette was low to the ground but Farrell thought the extra four or five feet should be enough. He jumped, reaching for the bottom rung of the ladder, and winced as he missed and his feet hit the roof of his car, probably denting it. He jumped again, this time getting a hand on the ladder. With a mighty heave, he thrust his other arm upward and then began to pull himself hand over hand until he could pull a leg up and stand.

The ladder to the water tower was about 200 steps long, and many of them were rotted through. Farrell had no time, so although he knew he should do this more carefully, he could only rush headlong up the ladder, hoping it wouldn't give under his weight, trying not to look down, not to think. Lucky he was an athlete. It had become his mantra as he climbed. He was strong, agile. He wasn't even out of breath. Lucky he was an athlete. A cracking sound alerted him, but before he could react, he was already swinging out over the abyss holding on with one hand, his feet dangling beneath him. Terror slid icy fingers into his bones, and he could feel himself going numb, losing his sense of his position in space.

The rung he was gripping might not hold his weight; he could already feel it giving way. Refusing to think, refusing to allow fear to have its way, he drove himself upward, and grabbed the next rung. Now he had two hands bearing his weight, but what about his feet? He pulled them in around the outer runners of the ladder and inched his hands to the outside as well. He could do it. He had to do it. He was an athlete. Slowly, he edged upward.

♦ ♦ ♦

Stokes was having a good time. For once the roles were reversed. Instead of them playing with him, he was playing with them. He had his knife out and pressed against that little bitch, Susan's, throat. With her in front of him, Jeffy couldn't shoot. This was fun. "Now, Jeffy, put down that gun or I'll cut her throat. It won't be as much fun as I planned, but . . . oh well . . . "

He could see Jeffy trembling. Was he scared? Angry? He didn't care. He just wanted to play the game the way it should have been played all those times when they'd ganged up on him and locked him up for days and days. It didn't look like Jeffy thought he was serious, so he dug the point of the knife in. Susan screamed. And there, he'd done it: Jeffy dropped the gun.

"Now, let her go!" Jeffy yelled.

"Okay," he said. "This is my favorite game."

CHAPTER FOURTEEN

As soon as Stokes let Amy go, Sean saw her rush toward him. He pulled her close and began to edge toward the opening in the tank wall. But Stokes was coming at him, his knife extended. He was laughing. "That's it. That's how we play."

Outside was a catwalk that went all the way around the tank. It was narrow and many of the planks were rotted through, leaving holes in the floor. Sean ran for the ladder, holding Amy's hand and pulling her after him. Suddenly, her foot broke through the wood and a hole opened up beneath her. She fell forward, screaming as her body hit the planking. The crack of another board seemed as loud as a gunshot. Sean was losing his grip on her hand, and threw himself to the floor to get another hand on her. But Stokes was quicker. He grabbed Amy under her shoulders and heaved, pulled her out of the widening hole in the floor and carrying her back inside.

"It's a little dangerous out there, Susan," he said. "You should be more careful."

From outside, Sean could hear her crying, pleading with that nutcase to let her go. Following the two of them back into the tank, he could see Stokes in the pool of light cast by the lantern. He leaned forward, caressed Amy's cheek and kissed her on the forehead. Sean wanted to kill him, but he'd lost the gun. A length of rope lay on the floor a little closer to Stokes. It had probably been used to tie Amy. Sean moved forward stealthily and picked it up, then continued on, keeping in the shadows against the curve of the wall.

As he moved, the angle at which he could see Stokes changed until his back was to him and Amy was no longer visible.There's nothing else to do, Sean thought, and jumped, landing on the man's back with the length of rope around his neck.

Stokes let go of Amy and turned to battle with Sean. He was much bigger and stronger than the boy, and easily pulled the rope from his hands. Then he turned to face him, and threw a left hook that knocked Sean to the ground. Sean held his hands up to defend his face as Stokes sat astride him and pulled his knife out. Sean looked at the deadly point being lowered to his chest and knew total and inescapable despair. He had lost and both he and his sister would lose their lives.

But a flicker of movement behind Stokes fanned the flames of hope. Amy had the gun.

"I have the gun!" she shouted.

Stokes turned his body to look at her, at the wildly wavering gun in her hand. Sean wondered if she'd even have the strength to pull the trigger.

"Do you think you can shoot me before I drive this knife into his heart?" the man said.

A loud shot reverberated through the rounded space of the tank, and Sean seized the opportunity, trying to roll out from under Stokes and his knife. Amy tried again, and Sean could see that the bullet has ripped through his enemy's shirtsleeve, but no blood spurted. She'd missed. Twisting away, he was on his belly when he felt the knife tear through the leather of his jacket. He was pinned to the floor! Struggling frantically to get his arms free, he could see Stokes reaching for the rope lying just within reach.

The madman laughed when another shot rang out and didn't make contact. Sean writhed and struggled but it was no good. In a few economic movements, Stokes had him trussed like a chicken, his arms tied to his legs. He was powerless once again. The click of the trigger falling on an empty chamber made him struggle anew.

Stokes pulled the knife out of the floor. "Come on, Susan," he said. "He can't help you. You'll be nice to me now, won't you?"

Sean watched helplessly as Stokes approached Amy. She screamed as he held her tightly with one hand and carefully cut her shirt off with his knife.

"No! Don't! Don't!" Amy screamed.

"That's it, Susan. Scream."

◆ ◆ ◆

The view from the air was nothing like the view from the ground, and at five hundred feet both Marilyn and Chessman realized they had no idea where to find the old water tower.

"Where is it?" Marilyn screamed into the headphones.

Chessman threw up a hand in answer, and continued to study the puzzle that was the ground.

So far the only landmarks he could make out were the highway and the river. And in the darkness, he wouldn't swear to the river.

Marilyn pointed. "I think it's that way!"

Chessman had no idea either way, so he headed the helicopter in that direction. It was as good as any.

◆ ◆ ◆

Farrell came over the top of the ladder and crouched down, the screams of the little girl lancing through him. Quickly, he edged toward the light coming through a large crack in the wall of the tank. Sticking his head inside, he could see Stokes poised over Amy about twenty feet away, his knife gliding across her chin.

"Stokes!" Farrell yelled as he stood up inside the tank. "Let her go, Stokes. It's over."

Stokes looked up, startled. But he seemed to recover quickly. "Oh no, it's just beginning, Dad," he said. Pulling Amy in front of him, he shielded his body as Farrell moved closer.

"Get out of here, now!" Stokes said. "Or I'll kill her."

"Let her go!"

Stokes grabbed Amy under her arms and swung her out over the abyss in the middle of the tank, and Farrell stopped abruptly, backing off. Stokes glared at him, teetering to keep his balance, stepping backward to get a better footing. Farrell waited until he'd pulled her back toward the flooring and set her down. Then he lunged, catching Stokes below the knees and knocking him over.

The man was strong, and Farrell fought with all his power to stop him. Stokes pushed the knife toward his throat. They were immovable object against irresistible force until the balance was tipped and Farrell had the upper hand. For a moment, he thought he'd disarm him, but then Stokes's knife drove into his leg and Farrell rolled, almost falling into the hole in the middle of the tank. Stokes lunged at him again, and he scrabbled out of the way, getting to his feet and limping for the hole that led to the outside catwalk.

Behind him he could see Stokes coming on, rage distorting his features and the bloody knife held in his fist. Farrell could still feel the shock of that steel in his leg. He moved to the side of the opening in the wall, and took a deep breath. When Stokes came through he tried to use the man's own forward momentum to drive him over the edge of the catwalk, but there wasn't enough momentum. Stokes turned before he'd reached the edge and drove his knife toward Farrell's chest. He moved quickly and the blade hit the outside wall of the tank instead of him. Taking advantage of the moment, Farrell hit Stokes's arm with all his might, and threw a hook to his upper body. The man was undaunted. He yanked the knife from the wood and raised it to meet Farrell's next thrust.

Farrell threw himself aside, rolling on the planking and coming up into a crouch. The floor gave beneath him and he fell; one of his legs dangled in space.

Stokes could see that he was helpless. "Now it's your turn, Dad!" he cried. Lifting the knife, he held it by the tip and brought his arm back for the throw that would end Farrell's life.

Out of the corner of his eye, Farrell saw Amy, wide-eyed, watching through the opening. Sean was behind her, already starting to step into the fray. But there was no time. Before the kid could move, that knife would be in his chest.

◆　◆　◆

It was like a scene from Hell. Wallace struggled, but several men were holding him. There were bodies strewn on the concrete, prison guards mostly. He didn't know if they were dead or injured. Sirens wailed. Lights flashed.

"Hang him!" one of the rioters shouted.

"Hell no! A rope is too good!"

"We should shoot him!" someone else screamed.

Bright lights highlighted the faces of his captors, and he thought that if he lived, he would never forget the horror that he saw in them. Had he been completely wrong about people all his life?

He heard a car door slam, and then Braun stepped into the space the others made for him. The beam of car headlights lit him from behind. "Get other cars!" the former prison guard ordered. "We'll take care of this guy once and for all."

Wallace's body shifted as other hands replaced the ones holding him. He struggled anew trying to take advantage of any momentary weakness in the muscular barrier standing between himself and freedom. A leg was free! He kicked out at someone, and felt the satisfactory thud as he connected. Then other hands held him once again.

He couldn't see behind the brights of the headlights, but he could hear as the trunk was opened. Then Braun stood in the lights again, heavy chains held in his hands. He handed these out to some of the men.

"Bring him over here," he ordered.

Struggling helplessly, Wallace was half carried, half dragged toward Braun who was busily readying the chains for use. Wallace's anguish was answered by a large grin. "Remember me, Doc?" the man said.

Wallace met his eyes and then tried once more to escape as Braun wrapped a chain around his wrist, securing it with a padlock. Braun kept the chain taut as he pulled it and wrapped it around the bumper of his car.

Wallace looked at the others, at their gleaming, fascinated eyes. He knew it was over. Would they actually do this? Other cars drove forward, and backed themselves into position. Could he die now? Could he simply leave his body now before this thing was done? He screamed in fear, wet himself as his other arm and his two legs were secured by chains and tied to the bumpers of three other cars. Someone laughed. He was stretched out between four cars. Die! He screamed inside himself. Die now!

◆ ◆ ◆

Farrell watched Stokes' hand as if in slow motion as he drew it back to make his throw. He saw Sean lunge toward the man and knew it was too late. He saw the knife reach the arc of the throw, the point of release, when the sudden unlikely noise of a helicopter filled the air. A chopper rose at a crazy angle toward the top of the tower impossibly close to them. Stokes's arm, ready to release the knife was suddenly missing from his body as the blades of the chopper cut into him, and flung his armless body into the night. In the cabin of the chopper, Farrell could just glimpse Marilyn's terrified face as the machine tilted on its side and almost spilled her into the abyss as well. Chessman struggled at the helm to bring the giant machine under control.

But Farrell had other problems. The catwalk seemed to be disintegrating around him. He grabbed one rotted board after another, but couldn't get a grip on anything solid. Then Sean, lying on the boards as if on thin ice, extended his arms, screaming over the noise of the chopper. "Grab my hands!"

Farrell could feel his body slipping into space. There was nothing else to grab onto but the slim chance that this boy could hold his weight long enough for him to grab something solid. He seized those hands and heaved, a prayer on his lips.

Miraculously, he crouched once more on the not-so-terra-firma of the catwalk, and watched the aircraft tilting crazily first one way and then the other as Chessman tried to get it close enough to hover. The blades swept close and Farrell knew that wasn't going to work. They might end up like Stokes if they weren't careful.

"Go down!" he shouted, pointing downward. "Go down!"

Chessman nodded, and the helicopter, thank God, moved away from the tower and began to descend. Farrell breathed, realizing that for several moments, he'd forgotten to do that. It was over. They'd simply wait for someone to get them off the tower.

A loud crash and the sudden shock wave that shook the structure, nearly toppling them all off their narrow perch, put an end to that idea.

Turning, Farrell limped over to where Sean stood holding his weeping sister. The boy looked up at him. "Why?" he said. "Why?"

Farrell didn't have an answer to that right now. "Sean, listen to me. It's not over, not yet. We still have to get your sister down that ladder before this whole thing collapses."

"Why does it have to be like this?"

Farrell put an arm around him. "I don't know. But I hope. I hope that we can do better. Help me with Amy, Sean. She's too frightened to climb down without our help.

Sean looked at Amy, and Farrell watched as the boy's face softened. He knelt beside his sister and drew her into his arms. She rested her little head on his shoulder. "Come on, Amy. We're almost home."

Amy threw her arms around Sean, and he hugged her tightly.

"Come on," Farrell called from the ladder. "Come over here. I'll go first," he explained to Amy, "so if you slip, I can catch you. All right?"

Stepping onto the ladder and going down a few rungs, he tried to ignore the bleeding of his leg while he waited for Sean to coax Amy to take the first step.

"Don't look down, Amy!" Farrell called. "Just look straight ahead. I'm right here to catch you."

Amy whimpered. "I want my mother."

"Your mother is waiting for you, honey. Just keep moving so your brother can come down too."

Amy took a cautious step and the three of them began the long trek down to the ground.

Halfway down, Farrell lost all feeling in his injured leg. It would hardly support his weight and he was having to bear more and more weight on his hands. Without that leg he had to hop from rung to rung and every time he did, he was terrified that it would crack under him. His arms were doing most of the work, but the rungs were getting slippery with the blood from his leg.

Above him, Amy cried out, "It's blood! It's blood!"

"Amy! Amy!" he called up to her. "It's my blood. Stokes cut me with the knife, but I'm okay. Just keep moving down. We're almost there."

They were almost there, just another thirty or forty feet to go. His useless leg hanging, Farrell hopped to the next lower step, taking most of his weight in his shoulders and arms. But the rung broke, and he dropped. Hanging by his arms, he realized several rungs were missing and he couldn't reach the next one with his foot. And if he couldn't, neither could the children. He was hanging as he called for the two kids above him to stop. Grabbing tightly onto the rung with one hand, he released the other, swinging out into space as his free hand sought the next higher rung. Then he pulled himself up and fought to gain his balance. Once he was secure, his injured leg thrown over the rung and one arm wrapped around the side of the ladder, he spoke to the two children above him. "Amy. Sean. Listen, there's a couple broken rungs. I'm going to help you get down. Amy, come down two steps and take my hand." He waited, hoping she wouldn't freeze. "That's it. Okay. Hold onto the side of the ladder with your other hand

and I'm going to lower you down. You can do it. Come on baby. It's just like the playground. Come on. You're almost there."

Amy cried as he lowered her in space, wiggling around to find a foothold. Farrell's hand was locked on her wrist, but if she didn't stop moving so much he'd lose her! "Amy! The rung is right there. Move your foot forward a little."

Breathlessly, he held on as Amy, still crying, took his instructions and found a toehold. With Farrell's assistance, Sean followed her. They edged their way down as Farrell extricated himself from his position and grabbing onto the sides of the ladder, slid down to that life-saving rung. They were almost there. Thirty feet more. Twenty-five.

He heard the sirens beneath them and saw the lights of the fire truck. Would they get into place in time? Before his arms gave out?

A voice called out. "Come on James! Come on!" Marilyn. Then he heard a scream as the leg of the tower cracked, his hands slipped, and he fell.

♦ ♦ ♦

Wallace was still conscious despite his wish to die instantly and not be torn apart. Braun's voice screamed, "Let's go!"

He heard the car engines rev up and felt the tautness in his body as they started to move. A shot rang out and one of the chains snapped, releasing one of his legs.

♦ ♦ ♦

In the helicopter, Paul Trevino looked at the scene beneath him. He leaned out of the chopper with a megaphone. "Break it up! This is the police!"

The marksman next to him had been given his orders, and Trevino watched as he aimed at another one of the chains on

Wallace. But the helicopter shifted and he aborted the shot. The next one went true, hitting the chain on Wallace's right arm.

On the ground, Trevino could see police wearing gas masks rushing into position. Tear gas flooded the area and many rioters were being captured and herded toward the vans. Three of the drivers of the cars that were going to draw and quarter Wallace got out of their vehicles and surrendered. But Wallace was still stretched out between two cars with a chain on his left arm and one on his right leg.

The marksman aimed at another chain, but police battling one of the rioters got in the way and he couldn't squeeze off the shot. "Get out of the way!" he screamed, though he knew that no one could hear him.

Trevino, horrified, watched as the driver of the last car leaned out his window and yelled at his surrendering compatriots, his face murderous with rage. Then he stepped on the gas. Wallace screamed. A shot rang out and the driver's head hit the windshield, sending the car into a spin.

CHAPTER FIFTEEN

DECEMBER 5TH – 10:12 AM

"The United States is a land of law and order, and it is still true here that an individual is innocent until proven guilty. John Wallace had been falsely accused, and he was subsequently acquitted of any wrongdoing. The real murderer of those two unfortunate boys is dead. Yet, Dr. Wallace suffered unspeakably because of the existence of a law which allowed our citizens to believe that it was all right to take justice into their own hands. While due process may at times be slow and cumbersome, it does what it should. That is, it keeps convicted criminals incarcerated and prevents the innocent from being executed for crimes they did not commit. The mob does not rule in America and the purpose of the law is not vengeance.

"While brutality and violence have always been a part of human history, we have made progress. We no longer cut off the right hands of thieves, or remove the tongues of liars. We no longer find our entertainment at public beheadings and hangings. We are more merciful, more humane than that. The so-called Eye-for-an-Eye law returns us to a medieval age that is barbaric, and metes out cruel and inhuman punishment. This court finds Texas Statute number 5884 in violation of the Eighth amendment of the United States Constitution and hereby declares it null and void."

The Supreme Court justice who had made the statement banged his gavel, and all the judges stood and filed out.

◆ ◆ ◆

John Wallace was one of the first to exit the courtroom. No one stepped in his path as he limped down the aisle toward the double doors, the metal cane in his right hand helping to support his weight. Few of the spectators met his eyes or looked at the sleeve of his jacket pinned up against the left side of his body. His eyes were haunted, looking as if he'd walked through the fires of Hell and somehow survived. He looked neither left nor right.

James Farrell was also limping and his arm was in a sling, but he looked happy as he met Wallace in the aisle and captured him in a bear hug. "We did it, John!" he said.

Wallace smiled, enjoying the sight of the tee-shirt that Farrell's open jacket had revealed: "An Eye-for-an-Eye makes the whole world blind," it said. "We did indeed."

Farrell's arm dropped from his shoulder as they both stepped through the doors to meet the horde of reporters waiting for them.

Wallace didn't stop, nor did Farrell. They brushed past the microphones and wended their way through the crowd toward the exit. Suddenly, Wallace halted. Across the hall stood Lindsey, and he almost cried out. Her face was as lovely as ever, and he knew that he'd betrayed her. But which was worse? His betrayal or hers? In his hour of need, she had sided with the enemy. He hated her for that. Though he loved her still. He looked at her eyes pleading with him to forgive and searched inside for the power to do so. But all he found was despair and regret. He had seen the depths to which humans could descend, and he would never again trust enough to love one of them. Oh he still had his ideals, but that was all he had. His innocence was gone forever. Turning away from Lindsey, he walked on.

"John!" she cried. "I'm sorry."

He could hear her crying fading into the distance, and then it didn't matter anymore.

The crowd of reporters made way for Glen Morgan of Titan Networks. The moment couldn't have been set up better.

"Congratulations, gentlemen," Morgan said. "You've won a great victory." Never one to miss a chance at publicity, Morgan directed the rest of his speech toward the microphones. "Vengeance is, after all, best left in God's hands." Magnanimously, he offered his hand to Wallace.

Wallace did not pick up his cue. Instead he moved aside to let Marilyn Hunter in between himself and Farrell. She took a sheaf of papers from inside her jacket and placed them in Morgan's outstretched hand.

"How fortunate that you were here," she said. "It saves me the trouble of hiring someone to serve you."

Morgan frowned and opened the papers.

"It says," Farrell said, "that John Wallace here is suing your company for one billion dollars in damages. It seems you paid a tidy sum to have him framed."

"You can't do this!" exclaimed the media tycoon. "That could put us out of business!"

"We certainly hope so," Wallace smiled.

"Of course, it's nothing compared to the criminal case that the State has against you." Marilyn was clearly enjoying her role in this. Standing next to her, Wallace could almost feel her elation as Morgan's face went pale.

"Ginny Ormond can't seem to stop talking. She wants to stay out of jail," Farrell said. "I don't think she'll be acting as your corporate counsel on this one." Signaling to two police officers waiting on the sidelines, he stepped aside and let them cuff Morgan.

The reporters were stunned. They went into overdrive, badgering Wallace, Farrell and Marilyn as they hurried toward the exit. Farrell dispatched them with a promise to hold a press conference, and the three finally reached the sunshine.

Farrell stood at the top of the courthouse steps and grinned. "Sometimes, being the DA is the best job in the world."

Wallace nodded. "Thank you for finally choosing sides on this, James. We couldn't have done it without your help."

Farrell clapped him on the back, and watched as he limped down the steps, his painfully lopsided body a reproach to anyone who ever advocated violence.

◆ ◆ ◆

"Farrell?" Marilyn said.

He looked at her, really seeing her for the first time in a long time. "Hunter?"

"How was Amy this morning?"

Farrell smiled. "She's coming along. One man tried to murder her . . . another one saved her. We can't all be bad.

His leg didn't hurt that much anymore, but stairs were still difficult. He held onto the rail as they descended.

"And what about you, James?" she asked.

"Me? Hmmm. Much as I'd like to go back to my old life, I can't. I've lost it . . . the edge . . . the desire to cut down, to punish, to make people pay . . . I thought I'd try the other side once my term is up, or maybe even no side. Maybe John Wallace and I will work on campaign reform . . . get the government back into the hands of the people. Or maybe we'll take on other violations of our constitutional rights . . . I'm also planning to take up flying."

"Flying!"

"Yeah, I've got a hankering to explore the sky." Farrell stopped at the bottom of the stairs and studied Marilyn's concerned eyes. "So many things to do next."

Marilyn leaned against the railing. "I know something you could do next," she said, her voice warm and suggestive.

Farrell looked her over and she looked good. "That's right. Don't I have a raincheck for something or other?"

She smiled and he pulled her close. Her lips were as warm and inviting as they'd been that night so long ago.

"You didn't get it in writing," she whispered into his ear.

"Oh no. You mean I have to do all that work all over again?"

"What work?" she joked.

"Oh you know. Coming to the rescue, solving crimes, saving innocent children, climbing condemned water towers. . . "

"Upholding justice."

"Yeah. Righting wrongs, walking on rotten catwalks, falling. You know. Your basic hero stuff."

Marilyn laughed, kissing his cheeks, his nose, his lips. "Nah, you might get hurt. Who needs a contract anyway?"

◆ ◆ ◆

Paul Trevino sat in a dark corner of his living room drinking a beer. He was waiting for the other shoe to drop. It was only a matter of time. At Farrell's insistence, he'd resigned as police chief. Soon, he knew he'd be arrested.

A car pulled up to the house, and he got up to look out the window. It was a police car. So the time had come. He opened the door and faced the young cop who had come to get him.

He'd been that young once. He'd been as tall and straight, as whole as this young officer. He'd had ideals and had thought that he would help to make a better world. Briefly, he wondered how he'd gone so far astray. How had it come to this?

The cop reached out a hand that held not cuffs but a letter, and Trevino hesitantly took it from him. "Mr. Trevino," he said. "I have a letter from the DA. He insisted I deliver it to you personally."

Trevino backed into the house and shut the door. Feeling older than he'd ever felt before, he limped over to his chair. His prosthesis was hurting today. A flash of John Wallace as he'd last seen him, with chains on his leg and arm flashed through his mind. He'd been responsible for that. Though he'd blamed Wallace for years for the loss of his own leg, he now realized that it was the war that had taken it, not Wallace. Not the medic who hadn't been able to save it. The war.

He'd envied him throughout high school and then after he'd lost his leg, he'd hated him. And now, all he could see was how he'd made one mistake after another, one egotistic decision after another. Taking a deep breath, he tore open the letter. It was time to know his fate.

"Sometimes, the good guys win," Farrell wrote. "I'm sorry you were on the wrong side because I will always think of you as a good man. I won't indict you. For what? For being an old fool? You've lost your job; you've lost your pension; you've even lost the girl."

"Ginny," Trevino thought. "Oh Ginny."

"You did a terrible thing, and almost cost a good man his life, but then if you weren't there to stop the riot . . . who knows? Maybe you also saved his life. I know that if it were up to you, you'd have no mercy, but then, I'm not you. And I don't want to become you. If I've learned anything from this, it's that mercy is all that stands between us and Hell."

Trevino, his heart full of feelings and images that would haunt him for the rest of his days, put his head in his hands and wept. Great wrenching sobs filled the emptiness of his body, his house, and his life.

May 21ST - 1:22 PM

Farrell wound up the pitch and threw the ball. He was still an athlete. Though it had taken some time for him to recover his strength and agility, he had it back now. He knew it because the ball went exactly where he'd placed it. The batter hit it hard and fast and Farrell backed up and caught the ball after it bounced. Turning, he raced for first and tackled Sean before he could make the base. The boy went down and they both lay in the grass laughing at themselves.

Sean had been transformed by his experience, proving that in some mysterious way even the worst events can produce something good. Farrell grinned at the kid and started to get to his feet. But Sean grabbed his legs and pulled them out from under him.

It was a shock to be on the ground again, but he rolled onto his back and looked at the blue sky. Sean, lying next to him, punched him lightly on the arm. They laughed at how good it was to be alive. From the stands, they could hear their girls— Marilyn, Sean's mother, and Amy—laughing along with them.

◆ ◆ ◆

The city is full of different people living different lives. Even as one is filled with joy, another is suffering unspeakable anguish. While one grieves, another sings. It was the way of the world. The way of all humans, and the reason why joy is always so fleeting. Until all could know love, each in their own way, and all could know freedom and redemption, earth would always be earth, and heaven would always be somewhere else.

The place was a dive. It was filled with smoke and sin. In this bar, lost men sat drinking in the middle of the day, watching women, ruined very young, as they took off their clothes to earn a living.

A young man sat at the bar, holding a swizzle stick between his fingers. Rolling it back and forth, he watched one of the dancers grind her body in time to the music. The swizzle stick moved up, thrusting. The other hand lifted a bottle from the bar and took another swig. The face looked blank, but the eyes seemed to leak lust, anger, and depraved fascination. Behind his eyes, Peter Sennet was remembering the feel of a knife driving into the flesh of Sam-the-Slasher. He was remembering the sweet pleasure of being in absolute control over the life of another. And a part of him craved that feeling again. Which one would it be? The blonde? Or the bitch in the blue robe? Which one?